Bitterness and conscience were competing for Joe Elliott, pulling him back and forth on a tightrope strung between right and wrong. Joe was a jailbird, and his neighbors wouldn't let him forget it; he'd tried to atone by working hard and staying clean, but constant insults and humiliations were pushing him nearer and nearer to breaking point.

The straw bent when Joe heard that a member of the Reb Beecher gang was hurt badly during a bank robbery. His half brother Bart—one of the very few people who had ever tried to help Joe—was in that gang, and if he was the one who was hurt, Joe wanted to be with him . . .

As he rode out toward the outlaw trail, Joe knew he was jeopardizing his chances for freedom; bitterness pushed him one way, his conscience pulled him another. Which way would he go?

REBEL TRAIL

D. B. Newton

GUNSMOKE

First published in the UK by Collins

This hardback edition 2008
by BBC Audiobooks Ltd
by arrangement with
Golden West Literary Agency

ISBN 978 1 405 68207 7

British Library Cataloguing in Publication Data available.

Printed and bound in Great Britain by
Antony Rowe Ltd., Chippenham, Wiltshire

FOR

JANET

REBEL
TRAIL

CHAPTER I

Suppertime at the Quitman farm began with prayer. That didn't mean any hurried, formal blessing, either, but a regular full-length spellbinder from the old man that seemed to go on and on, endlessly, while the dishes his niece would have worked so hard to put steaming on the table gradually cooled out and lost their savor. It was always an ordeal for the hired hand, Joe Elliott, who came to his meals starved from the long day's toil, and hollow to the soles of his heavy work shoes.

Listening to the steady drone issuing from that gray, chopped-off fan of beard, Joe would let his look run around the sodhouse kitchen like a trapped animal on a tether—from whitewashed dirt walls and warped cottonwood flooring, up to the ceiling that was nothing more than muslin sheeting tacked directly to the rafters, on through the window to the gaunt skeleton of a windmill creaking away in windy Kansas dusk. And then his eye would settle on Mary Quitman's still, bent head, across the table; wistfully he'd ask himself what went on under that soft, dark hair, that she wore cropped short and clubbed behind her neck with a bit of scarlet ribbon. He could scarcely resist, sometimes, reaching out a hand and touching it.

What would she think or do, he often wondered, if he ever dared try it? More to the point was what her Uncle Abel would do—this hard old man, whose cold stare never let Joe Elliott forget for a moment that he'd still be serving time in Lansing Prison, except for Quitman's fine Christian charity in interceding for him and taking his parole. . . .

Supper was usually accompanied by a running commentary on whatever had been done that day, and on the hired man's many shortcomings. Tonight, though, there was something else on Quitman's mind. "Well, Joseph," he said, when the last amen had been spoken; his tone stayed young Elliott in the act of reaching for the platter of roasting ears. "I suppose you'd be interested in the bulletin I saw, tacked up outside the *Clarion* office in town this afternoon."

Joe Elliott said cautiously, "I would?"

The pale eyes rested fully on him, behind blue-veined and heavy lids. "There was a train robbery over east of Wichita last evening. Somebody tried to hold up the Santa Fe Special. According to reports, it was Reb Beecher's crowd."

"Reb Beecher!" Mary Quitman gasped, and her fork clattered. "Are you sure? Why, it's more than a year since anyone's so much as heard of him!"

"I don't doubt he's been lying low somewhere, down in Indian Territory with the rest of that scum. Anyway, last night he was recognized. And they killed one of his men."

Joe Elliott swallowed to clear a throat suddenly gone dry. "You didn't happen to notice—which one?"

The deep hollows of the old man's cheeks gathered shadow as his mouth drew down. "No," he said curtly, "I didn't. Far as I can see it makes no difference. I just pray the Lord they kill them all, and be rid of them!"

Though she lived in terror of her uncle's moods, Mary

nevertheless found courage now to protest. "How can you talk like that? As though they weren't human!"

"Are they? I'd say mad dogs was a better name! But of course, I can't expect Joseph to agree with me." Gaunt, work-hardened hands scooped a turnip onto his plate. "He probably wishes he was back with them, right now—with the law hunting him!"

"Who says so?" Joe retorted, stung.

"You don't fool me. Human nature doesn't change that quick—at least, not for the good! Not when a man's got bad blood in him."

"Damn it, there's nothing wrong with my blood!"

The hooded eyes kindled. "You can't deny it put you in Lansing Prison before you were twenty!" He added, too softly, "If you'd like to go back there and finish out the rest of your sentence—I'm sure it can be arranged!"

"Uncle Abel!" cried Mary, horrified. The color was drained from her fine-boned, gentle features. "You're always talking about sending him back. You shouldn't even joke about such a thing!"

"I'm not sure anyone's joking. Sometimes, I don't think this young man appreciates the chance he's been given, to make up for a bad beginning. I don't think he shows proper gratitude for the advantages of hard work and a good Christian home!" The pale eyes considered Joe thoughtfully. "What do you say, Joseph? Shall we consider the subject closed? Shall we try to enjoy this meal the Lord had seen fit to provide—and not raise our tongue against our benefactors?"

Joe Elliott's gaze dropped before that searching stare. The taste of humility was bad in his mouth, but he made himself say, "Yes sir."

"Very good. And we'll have no more talk about this matter. I'd prefer never to hear mention of any of those outlaws in my house again!"

The quiet, after that, was better; but not much. Joe Elliott's

3

appetite had vanished. The good supper Mary had toiled over was as tasteless as cardboard and as hard to swallow; suddenly he'd had too much of the oppressive stillness and the trapped heat of the sodhouse kitchen. The chair screeched on warped cottonwood floorboards as he pushed abruptly to his feet.

Abel Quitman's deep voice rumbled warning: "I think you'd better sit down and finish your meal, Joseph."

But he didn't wait. "I'm not hungry," he said gruffly, and was already on his way to the door.

He felt better when it slammed behind him. Alone, he discovered that his legs were shaking. He walked out to the iron water tank and stood beside it, trembling with emotion, listening to the steady, complaining creak of the windmill and the splash of water running from the pipe.

Dusk was coming down, now, upon the endless Kansas prairie; there were a few stars already, though daylight still lay against the flat edge of the sky. Over in the pen, Quitman's turkeys were making a querulous racket as they settled to roost on the sides of an old wagon box. The steady wind that ran along the flats was warm yet from the summer day, but it felt cold as it struck Joe's body. His shirt, he realized, was stuck to him with sweat.

He knew it wasn't because he felt any particular concern for Reb Beecher. Not that scarred gray wolf of a man—that anachronism—still waging, singlehanded, a war with the North that had ended twenty years ago. To Joe, there was no doubt but he was crazy. "Rebel" he called himself, and he'd gone on writing the name in blood and fire across this Kansas Border country, even though the rest of Quantrill's guerrillas were long since dead and scattered.

Once there'd been the Youngers, coughing out their lungs now in a Minnesota prison. There'd been Jesse James, struck down by a traitor's bullet two years ago, over in Saint Joe across the Missouri. Today, there remained only Reb

4

Beecher—still hiding out in Indian Territory and carrying on the fight alone—still hating the Jayhawkers and all his other ancient enemies.

Sooner or later, Federal marshals or the Pinkertons were bound to cut him down. Maybe it would be some county sheriff, in some obscure Kansas town, who'd put a bullet into Reb during one of his mad-dog raids and leave him to spill out his blood in the dust.

But it wasn't any such thought that held Joe Elliott motionless here, with the questions buzzing inside his head like angry bees.

One of Reb Beecher's gang had died in the train job east of Wichita; so old Quitman had told him. But—which one?

It couldn't have been Bart Dolan. Oh God, no! he thought. Not Bart! But one way or another, he was going to have to know. He had to find out!

He didn't ask permission to ride into town. If the answer had been no, he'd have gone anyway; better, then, just to take off, rather than have to flout an order. He headed with determination toward the barn.

It was typical of Quitman that he and his niece still lived in a crumbling soddy, while the barn that housed his stock was new, built of sawed lumber. Joe's room was there, in a partitioned corner, furnished with a lamp and a bunk and table and chair. It had a rusty space heater, too, that was little use when winter blew at the cracks in the siding, and the nailheads in the wall would be hoared with frost when he woke of a morning.

He changed into his town clothes, such as they were, and hastily threw saddle and gear onto his old roan gelding and led him outside. Over at the house, lamplight shone golden yellow in the kitchen window. A shadow moved across the light—that was Mary, going on with her evening chores. He watched a moment, motionless.

After that he mounted, turned the old horse in the direction of Union City, and touched him up with a kick.

It wasn't yet full dark when he reached town. Lamps burned through the shadows piled against blocky wooden buildings, while the wide street's dust reflected the fading sky like dull, beaten silver. The place lay quiet in a soundless evening, not ready yet to stir from the crushing, day-long heat.

The *Clarion* office was closed tight, and Joe didn't know where to look for the editor. But the notice Quitman had mentioned seeing was thumbtacked to a bulletin board right outside the door; Joe was digging a match from the pocket of his sweat-faded blue work shirt, as he swung off the roan for a look.

He read the scrawled message twice through by matchlight. Time and place were given—6:23 P.M., July 28, 1884: Yesterday evening. The engineer and express guard of the train had definitely identified Reb Beecher as the leader of the men who flagged it down. One raider had been killed. That was every scrap of information to be worked out of it.

At least it didn't come right out and *say* it was Bart. And it would, wouldn't it? he argued with himself, anxious to believe. Why, it would be almost as big news as if old Reb Beecher himself had finally gone to meet whatever gods he'd served during all these smoky years. Bart Dolan had ridden with him longer than anyone. Surely, even this brief dispatch would have mentioned Bart by name.

The argument didn't help too much. He might not have been recognized at once. He could even have been shot up too bad to tell. Joe thought of that, too—and wished he hadn't. It was like a sick kind of gnawing deep inside. . . .

A voice spoke, right at his shoulder, and he came around too startled even to drop the match. Its flame made twin reflections in a pair of muddy eyes, lighted the dark face and

6

roached black mustache of Tod Grandy, who was foreman for one of the big ranches out on the Kansas prairie. He wasn't a lot taller than Joe but he was bigger in other ways. "Well!" he said, and an unpleasant grin lifted a corner of the mustache. "I guess somebody told you the news?"

"Yeah. Somebody told me."

Beyond the blocky shape, Joe glimpsed another man and recognized him as Rick Slaughter, the son of the man Tod Grandy worked for. He swallowed in a throat suddenly gone dry, because he knew he was in for a bad time. Why did he have to go and run into a pair like this—tonight of all nights?

"I could of guessed you'd be interested." An unlighted cigarette was pasted to Grandy's lower lip, bobbing as he talked. His arm shot out suddenly and he trapped Joe's hand in a hard squeeze, so that the bones grated painfully and he couldn't have opened his fingers. Deliberately, Grandy tilted his head forward and used the match to set his smoke afire.

He took long enough about it. Suddenly Joe yelled and was struggling to get free, but Grandy had a grip of steel. His victim broke away at last and stumbled back, shaking scorched fingers, as the match fell and guttered out.

"Damn you!" Joe was trembling with fury.

Grandy drew on his cigarette, letting its glow spread redly across the flat, big-nosed face. "Go ahead," he jeered. "Get tough! I been waiting a long time to see it!"

"Why, Grandy? Why do you have to keep devilin' me? What have I ever done to you?"

"Maybe I just want to see what it takes to make you stand up on your hind legs," Grandy said roughly. "A bank robber, they tell me—one of Reb Beecher's boys!" He snorted in contempt. "A punk farmhand, for *my* money. If you ever had any starch, that year at Lansing must have sweated it out of you! Ain't that about right?" And when Joe didn't answer, Tod Grandy flipped the fingers of one spread hand across his face. "*Ain't it?*"

It was not a hard blow—the merest flicking tap; but it shook Joe and brought up his clenched fists. He forced them down again, and spread them flat against the legs of shapeless overalls. He was glad then for the gathering dusk, so Grandy couldn't see the rush of angry blood into his face.

Rick Slaughter said, "Aw, hell, Tod! You won't get any fight out of him. Let's go on down to Kallen's. I want to look at some pasteboards—I feel lucky."

Joe looked at the man, leaning idly against an arcade roof prop. He figured Rick Slaughter really should have better things to do with his time than spend it helling around with his paw's tough foreman—throwing his paw's money away on cards and likker and the women in the hookshop at the east end of town. He'd never done a day's work in his life—never had to. He was big and soft and worthless; and to be treated with contempt by such as him was enough to rub salt into the raw wounds of anyone's spirit.

"Don't rush me," Grandy said. "I'm gonna see the color of this guy's spine—if he's got one. What about it, punk?"

"You want to make me fight you," Joe Elliott retorted in a voice that shook. "You want to push me until I can't back away any longer. You know what that would likely do to my parole—and I wish I could see what satisfaction it'd give you!"

Grandy only laughed, and despite the darkness Joe could almost see the sneer on his face. "You win, Rick," he agreed heavily. "I'm wastin' my time here. Let's go." But, in turning to leave, he laid a hand on Joe Elliott's shoulder and let him have a parting shove that drove him backward and slammed him, hard, against the rough plank wall of the *Clarion's* print shop.

CHAPTER II

"Hold your horses, there!" a new voice said sharply. "What's going on?"

Grandy and Slaughter, who had already started to move off along the dry and rattling sidewalk planks, paused and half-turned. "No trouble, Sheriff," Tod Grandy said pleasantly. "No trouble at all. We're just talking things over."

"That you, Grandy?" Sid Davis, the county sheriff, halted his hurrying stride. He peered at them through the dusk, identifying each in turn. "Rick?"

Rick Slaughter told him, "It's like Tod said. We were just passing the time of day."

The lawman's puzzled attention swung to Joe Elliott. A moment, only, the young fellow hesitated. "Yeah," he said gruffly. "That's right."

Davis plainly wasn't satisfied; it showed in the way he continued probing the dimly seen faces. But he wasn't going to accuse Morgan Slaughter's son, or his foreman, of lying to the law. "All right," he grunted finally.

"See you," Grandy said, and he and Rick Slaughter went

sauntering off together, in the direction of Kallen's Bird Cage a block away.

The night was waking up a little. Someone down at Kallen's had just dropped a nickel in the mechanical piano and it started up in the middle of a tune, its clatter falling like stones into the quiet. A horse and rig went by, raising bitter dust.

The stars had brightened as the sky grew dark. A sickle moon hung over the town, just above the peaked roof of Union City's barnlike bank. There, a light in the shaded office window indicated that Morgan Slaughter must be working late.

Sid Davis said, "You real sure it was like Grandy told me?"

"Said so, didn't I?" Joe was too humiliated to discuss it.

"For some reason, I had a notion he was picking on you." The sheriff waited but, when he got no answer, he gave it up. "Well, watch your step with him—that's all!" He added, "How's things out at Quitman's?"

"All right, I guess."

"And Mary?"

"She's fine."

The curtly spoken answers must have told the sheriff he wasn't going to break through the wall Joe Elliott had set up. Put off by the young fellow's manner, Davis said gruffly, "Evening, then." He turned and started back across the street to his office, and Joe watched him go.

But almost immediately the young man realized here was a source of information he might have made use of but had passed up, unthinking. He hesitated, knowing he hadn't behaved very well; but then the same urgent need that had brought him into town sent him after Davis, at an angle across the wide street toward the jail office.

When he paused hesitantly in the open door, Sid Davis was already slumped at ease in his barrel chair, under the cone of lamplight. He had a leg hiked up onto the corner of the desk, and both hands were folded across the beginning of a paunch. He raised a glance; black eyes, behind steel-rimmed glasses, raked Joe Elliott. They weren't too friendly.

"So!" the sheriff grunted. "Changed your mind, did you? Figure I'm worth talking to, after all?"

Joe swallowed the comment, knowing he had earned it. "I just thought I'd ask if you might have got a report on a train robbery, over east."

"Oh. That." He couldn't fool the sheriff; Sid Davis knew why he was interested, all right. But he only shook his head. "Afraid not."

"You don't know any more, then, than what's nailed up over there on the bulletin board?"

"Well, not a hell of a lot more. Way I get it, Beecher must have run into a regular hornet's nest. A detachment of the military was on one of the day coaches, bound for Fort Dodge —which I reckon was something the old fox never figured on. Soldiers had their sidearms with them. They chased him off without a dime."

This was considerably more detail than anyone had given him yet, and it all sounded bad. Joe touched his tongue to dry lips. "There—there was a man killed. You wouldn't happen to know—?"

Davis answered before he could finish. "Sorry, Elliott, I wouldn't. There was no names given."

"I see . . . Well—thanks anyway."

"Wait." Something in the voice stopped him as he was turning to go. He saw Davis take his foot off the desk, reach a long leg and kick out a chair. "Come in and set."

Joe hesitated, then reluctantly obeyed. Davis was in no hurry. He reached a smoke-blackened pipe off the desk, turned it over and over in his fingers as though he'd never rightly seen it before. He blew down the neck of it, and then abruptly tossed the pipe back onto the litter of the desk.

"Look!" he said. "You don't fool me. There's things bothering you—and as your parole officer, I got a right to know them. It'll fall on me if you should happen to make some kind of a mistake."

The young fellow's head jerked up; but he bit back the retort he came near making. Sid Davis, he supposed, was actually trying to help.

"Sounds to me," the sheriff said quietly, "like maybe Quitman's been making things tough for you."

"Oh, hell. No more'n usual, I reckon." Joe looked down at his hands—callused, broken-nailed, hardened by labor. "You know him as well as I do. He drives a man, but no more than he drives himself. There's enough of the dirt farmer in me to appreciate how he's managed to scratch a living for him and Mary out of that piece of hardpan." He shook his head. "If only he'd just take a rest, once in a while, from telling me how no-good I am! I get it from him; then I come to town and I get it—"

"There's some things you've got to expect," the sheriff reminded him, the black eyes intent behind the polished lenses. "Especially now that Reb Beecher's out stirring up the animals again. People in this part of the world have been scared of him for over twenty years. They know about your past connection with the gang. It's human nature that they'd start to get worked up. And if somebody like Tod Grandy, that figures he's pretty tough, takes it into his head to try proving it, at your expense—you just got to take it in your stride."

"You can't say I made any fuss about Grandy!" Joe retorted.

"I see. Then something *did* happen out there on the street just now! Well, I'm pleased that you let it go. Grandy's nothing—a loud-mouth who keeps his job with Morgan Slaughter only because he happens to know cattle. Forget him—and think about Joe Elliott.

"What is it that's really troubling you? It must be that Santa Fe job. You're worried about Bart Dolan. . . ." And when

Joe's expression showed he'd hit it square: "Is it true he's your brother?"

That got him a quick stare from the younger man. "Half brother," Joe Elliott said finally. "But I don't see how you know. I never told you nothing!"

"*That's* sure the truth!" Davis agreed dryly. "It was something Quitman let drop once. The difference in names, though—I sort of wondered."

"Quitman told you," Joe repeated, scowling. "He would! He says my being related to an outlaw is proof I'm headed for the dogs, because I got bad blood in me." He ran stubby fingers through his mop of sandy hair, and the hand was trembling. "It ain't so! My maw was a good woman, even if she didn't have much luck with either of her husbands. Or her sons, I guess," he added, in harsh self-condemnation.

"Whatever happened wasn't her fault. Tom Dolan was a drifter, a gambler. He ran out on her when Bart was little, wound up dead in the Idaho gold fields. So she tried again, and married an Ozark farmer—my paw. He used to beat her. Bart, too, till he was big enough to lay the old man out with a cottonwood limb and run away. I wasn't old enough to remember that, but I grew up hearing how Bart had turned outlaw—hearing Maw praying for him, every evening, till her dying day."

"She's dead, then?"

Joe nodded bleakly. "Took sick, a few years ago. Bart heard about it somehow and he sneaked back to the farm to see her, dodging the law every step of the way. I knew all about him, of course—the big brother I'd never seen, who was Reb Beecher's right bower and near as famous as Jesse James himself. I expected to see the devil, I reckon. And when he showed up he sure did look twice as big as most men. After he left again—with Maw in her grave, and nobody there on that farm but Paw and me—the place just wasn't big enough for me any more. I packed up and followed."

"And he and Reb Beecher took you into the gang," the sheriff finished. "And you had a part in that Emporia bank job . . ."

"I only held the horses," Joe corrected him. "Bart didn't even want me doing that much. But the gang was short-handed, and I was just a youngster eager to earn my keep."

Davis ignored his interruption. "The job went wrong and they all ran out on you; everyone else escaped. You were tried and you went to prison. You weren't quite twenty . . ."

There was silence, broken only by the jangle of the mechanical piano at Kallen's, and by the sawing of a cricket in a tree outside the open window. After a little of this, Joe Elliott shifted uneasily in his seat. He leaned forward, poised on the edge of the chair with palms on thighs. "Well?" he said roughly. "You finished with it?"

"Finished with what?"

"The sermon!"

He saw the sheriff's mouth tighten angrily. "Son, it wasn't meant to sound like preaching! I've been sort of interested in you, ever since Quitman come back from his visit to the parole board with you in tow. I always half-figured what he was really after was to get himself a hired hand, cheap—and at the same time have the satisfaction of thinking of himself as a soul saver. I been dubious from the start, whether he'd do you more harm than good!"

Abruptly he took his leg down from the desk. "But I'm damned if I'll be accused of preaching!" He swung around in his chair and picked up some papers. "Go your own way! You will anyhow, I reckon. But you just better see you keep out of mischief—and don't forget, Wednesday week is your day to come in and make your regular report."

Joe was on his feet, his cheeks burning. "I didn't mean—" he began and then broke off, scowling. "Never missed yet, did I?" He stood a moment looking down at the sheriff—waiting, thinking Davis must surely have something further to

14

say. But all he saw was the top of the man's balding head. The sheriff had dismissed him.

Joe Elliott choked back angry words, and he walked out of there.

CHAPTER III

Despite its fancy name, Kallen's Bird Cage was no gilded palace of pleasure. It was more like a long, narrow box, with a cheap bar along one side and a mechanical piano at the rear. The plaster was cracked down to the laths, in a few places, and the back bar mirror had never been the same after some drunk cowhand had put a bullet in the middle of it, one Saturday evening. There never seemed to be enough light in that room, and the air was bad; even the sawdust on the floor smelled sour.

But the beer Huck Kallen served up was wet, at least, and Joe Elliott stood moodily alone at one end of the dripping counter and ordered two in succession, drinking them slowly to put off the moment when he'd have to get on the roan and ride back to the monotony of the Quitman farm—and to the questions he knew would be waiting for him. There would be another row with the old man, no way out of it. And since he just wasn't equipped to face it yet, he dallied—even though he knew the later he stayed, the more of a storm he would face when he did go home.

Kallen was doing pretty good business. A fairly steady flow of customers moved through the batwings, and after an hour of listening to their talk Joe Elliott was pretty well abreast of all the local gossip, rumor, and opinion. Still, the name he heard the most often was Reb Beecher's—a man who'd been a legend for as long as that, didn't leap suddenly into the news without stirring up something of a storm.

But though Joe Elliott caught some coldly curious stares leveled at him, and saw men turn from their drinks to whisper to their neighbors, no one came near him or interrupted his solitary brooding. They knew him, all right; there wasn't anyone in a hundred miles but had heard the story about Abel Quitman's hired hand who'd ridden with Beecher. But these men weren't Tod Grandy; and they let him alone.

Luckily, Grandy himself wasn't here. Joe didn't know where he was spending his evening—like as not in the house at the east end of town with the red light over the door. But his friend Rick Slaughter sat at one of Huck Kallen's beige-topped card tables, deep in a game. A rotten poker player, Slaughter couldn't leave it alone; he normally ended up broke and plastering the town with IOUs that his old man had to make good. But tonight he'd said he felt lucky; and it certainly looked for once as though he couldn't lose for winning.

You could hear him crowing, above all the other racket— even above the clatter of the piano.

Among his victims were a trio of locals—the town doctor, the blacksmith, and Merl Cushman who owned the feed store. But it was a stranger who appeared to be the heavy loser, a slight, dark-haired man in a sack suit. "Stock buyer," Joe heard Kallen say in answer to someone's query about him. "Name of Lamb. Been in town a day or two; says he'll be going on tomorrow. I bet he's wishing he'd never stayed this long! The big boy is really taking him!"

"Lamb to the slaughter, huh?" his customer suggested, and Kallen laughed like he thought that was funny as hell.

Rick Slaughter's voice boomed loudly. "Little man across from me seems to think he's holding something. Well, little man, I'm just gonna call you and see what it is." The cattle buyer had pushed his whole remaining stack into the pot, and now Slaughter casually tossed in chips enough to match it. Merl Cushman and the doctor immediately threw in their hands, and only Lamb was left. With an air of confidence, he spread his cards.

Joe didn't see what he had, nor did he see what Rick Slaughter topped it with. He was watching Lamb's face, and he saw the life die on it. The stock buyer's head seemed to sink between his shoulders as he looked at the two hands. He laid both palms flat on the table in front of him; he shook his head and swore.

"Well, that cleans me!" he muttered. "Clear to the lint!" And he got to his feet.

Rick teetered back his chair and grinned up at him. "What's the matter, little man?" His voice carried over every other sound in the room. "Don't you like getting beat?"

The stranger glared at him; his mouth worked, and his face was drained of color. Finally he said hoarsely, "You loud-mouthed bastard! You can go to hell!" He gave his wire-enforced barrel chair a kick that slammed it into the wall, and he turned away. Slaughter's booming laugh followed him out of the Bird Cage.

"Sorehead!" said Rick. He looked around. "Who's for sittin' in?"

No one made a move. "Reckon I've had enough, myself," Doc Reasoner said quickly, and got out of his chair as though he was afraid one of those big, clumsy hands would try to grab and hold him there. Rick eyed him grinning.

"Scared out? Oh, well." He stretched, the chair creaked under his heavy, soft body; he yawned, as though bored with his winnings. "Cash me in, Merl," he said, and shoved to his feet. "And let's all have a drink. Huck, this is on me."

In the general stampede to the bar, Joe Elliott stood off the jostling elbows and drew farther apart and deeper into his own dark thoughts. Nobody here really liked Rick Slaughter, but they'd fall over themselves to drink his liquor. And, watching them, he had a revulsion of feeling. He'd always been on the defensive about Bart Dolan—about his own association with outlaws. But, dammit, suddenly he didn't feel like apologizing. Bart might be a thief, but he was twice the man of any in this bootlicking crowd. All at once Joe knew he wanted out of that place, out into the fresh and clean-smelling darkness.

A shotglass of whiskey had been set in front of him, along with the others, but he hadn't touched it. Now as he started to turn away his path was abruptly blocked; he looked up into Rick Slaughter's beefy, sweating face. "Ain't the likker I buy good enough for you, maybe?" Slaughter demanded, in his loud and carrying voice. Other talk ceased, though the piano kept up its mindless racket; Joe realized he was all at once the center of attention.

"No law says I have to drink it," he retorted coldly.

Then, apparently for the first time, Slaughter took a good look and recognized him. "The jailbird!" he exclaimed, his anger giving way to a wicked kind of amusement. "Reb Beecher's boy!" And he showed all his teeth in a grin.

Joe could almost see the thoughts working behind the vacuous blue eyes: Here was the yellowbelly he'd watched Tod Grandy pushing around. If Tod could get away with it, so could Rick Slaughter. And he'd never have a better audience than this saloon crowd, excited as they were over the news of the train robbery.

A hand rose and spread itself across Joe Elliott's chest, to pin him against the bar while men slid hastily out of the way. The hand was broad and soft, with a glinting of blond hairs across its back. Joe looked down at it, and then he lifted his stare to Slaughter's grinning face. He said, in a voice that he managed to keep steady and without trembling, "Take that thing off me."

Instead the palm shoved harder, pressing him back against the edge of the wood. And now, with his other hand, Slaughter reached and picked up the untasted drink—an amber jewel of reflected lamplight, engulfed in thick fingers. "You know what? I'm just gonna make you drink this whether you want to or not!"

Suddenly the glass was shoved into his face, slopping its contents. Joe twisted his head away, his lips set tight. He brought up a hand and chopped it hard against Rick Slaughter's wrist and sent the glass spinning.

A grunt of surprise broke from Rick Slaughter. He stared blankly a moment, empty hand still raised. Then his face turned red with anger. "Why, damn you!" The hand shaped itself into a fist and swung at Joe Elliott's head.

The blow had been plainly telegraphed, and Joe Elliott had plenty of time to twist away from it, pulling free of the hand that had had him pinned. Slaughter, thrown off balance, slammed into the edge of the bar, scattering glasses and bottles and jarring a yell from the startled bystanders. When he straightened and came around to face Joe, his features were twisted and ugly. "You goddamn' yellowbelly!" he shouted. "*Stand still!*"

Even yet Joe couldn't believe it was a fight. Rick Slaughter was heavy, ponderous, awkward; and he probably had never willingly stood and traded blows with anyone in his life. But maybe it was the unique chance he saw to play the bully before an audience, that drove him now. The fact that it wasn't turning out the way it should enraged him.

It probably never occurred to him that if he was bigger than his victim, he was also a lot softer. He'd forgotten that Joe—a farmhand—had just been putting in eighteen hours a day at the very hardest kind of labor.

He lunged at the younger man. Joe, hemmed in by the

crowd, couldn't fade out of the way this time. A wild swing grazed his cheek, bounced off his shoulder. Because it had Rick Slaughter's weight behind it, it hurt; but it didn't hurt much, because that weight was chiefly flab. What it did do was slip the leash on Joe Elliott's temper. All his unhappy resentments toward Quitman and Grandy and the sheriff, all his gnawing worry over the fate of Bart Dolan, welled up on the instant and burst in a Roman candle of angry energy. Nearly of its own accord his body responded.

Slaughter had caught his balance and was aiming a second blow. Joe had no trouble blocking it, and then his own right fist cocked and fired and he felt the knuckles bruise as they flattened Slaughter's lips against his teeth. The man staggered; pain and surprise mingled on his face. Joe took a step to close the distance and drove his left into the bulge of shirtfront just above Rick Slaughter's belt.

There was nothing to stop it and it seemed to sink in clear to the wrist. A bleat of agony gusted between the swelling lips. Slaughter clamped both hands over his belly and began to double forward. Too furious to stop himself, Joe swung again and caught his opponent on the forehead, snapping his head back hard. Slaughter stared at him with the bewildered eyes of a hurt child, and then his knees folded and he went down slowly and rolled over onto his side. He upset a dented brass spittoon, spilling its contents; it came to rest cuddled against his left cheek. He lay there and suddenly great sobs began shaking him.

Joe Elliott could only stare. He felt hands grab him by both arms, then, and lifting his head he looked blankly around. He realized the mechanical piano had ground to a stop, having finished working on the nickel someone had put in it. Suddenly the room was silent except for the sounds of men breathing and the scraping of a boot—and the whimpering of the man on the floor.

Disgust, and a kind of tired weariness, went through Joe

Elliott. "Oh, hell!" he muttered. "Let go—I ain't gonna hit the sonofabitch again!" He shrugged off the hands and looked at the knuckle he had split on one of Slaughter's front teeth. He ran a sleeve across his face, wiping it free of whiskey and sweat. "Look!" he said hoarsely. "You were all watching. You saw how it started. He shoved that glass in my face—he took the first swing . . ."

Stares, cold and unfriendly, met him; though he searched the crowd he could find no trace of sympathy.

Someone said sternly, "You refused to drink with him, Elliott! Man that by rights should be in prison . . ."

"Yeah," Merl Cushman echoed. "Makes you out to think you're better than the rest of us, maybe!"

Huck Kallen, behind the bar, growled, "Turning up his nose at my whiskey!"

Joe Elliott took a deep breath. "Now, wait!" he began, and stopped. He suddenly knew he'd be wasting breath to argue with them.

For all the show he was putting on, Joe couldn't believe Slaughter was really hurt. He'd left off his whimpering now and was sitting up with his back against the bar, still clutching his middle. Joe watched Doc Reasoner push through the crowd and go down on one knee. "Somebody lend me a hand, here," the doctor said. "Let's get him in a chair."

Huck Kallen had come around from behind the counter; he and another man stepped up to help with Rick Slaughter's limp weight. At first try his legs tangled with the chair and knocked it over.

Joe Elliott saw his chance. While everyone's attention was taken up in this way, he simply turned and walked out. He didn't think anyone even saw him go.

CHAPTER IV

In saddle, it occurred to him it might help to get to the sheriff first and put his version of the fight on record, before Sid Davis got it from another source. But the jail office was dark, so he rode on past and kept riding, and moments later had left the town behind.

Out here under the sultry stars, with heat lightning flickering away off on the horizon, he tried to look at the whole matter objectively. Maybe he was worrying too much. Maybe nothing would come of it. His record was good, wasn't it—no blot of any kind, in the year and a half of his parole.

But there was an uneasy, hollow feeling in his middle, just the same. He *would* have to go and get into trouble, tonight of all nights, with everyone worked up over Reb Beecher! It was going to be just too bad if the Slaughters, father and son, decided to make an issue of this incident —which was altogether too possible.

And then, there was Quitman. What would he say, when he learned that Joe had had the effrontery to go into town without asking permission, and had there got himself into a saloon brawl and was riding home with his very clothing soaked with raw whiskey? The old man might be of a mood to turn him over to the parole board himself. . . . He nearly panicked, then. But he got himself under control again and, with a fatalistic resignation, rode out the lonely miles.

The windmill had been turned off and the farm was quiet, the kitchen light making a single spark of brightness on the dark Kansas prairie. Starlight glimmered on Quitman's barbed wire and on the water in the tank. Joe sat a moment looking at the place, trying to summon up the words he would say. Nothing useful occurred to him, though; so he shrugged and rode in, directly to the barn.

He got down and led the old roan inside, without rousing anyone over at the house. Groping in the dark, his fingers from long familiarity quickly located the barn lantern on its nail; he popped a match and lit it, replaced the chimney and adjusted the wick. In the pale yellow wash of light, he turned to the old roan which had already walked into its stall. He was lifting the stirrup to get at the cinch, when a creaking of the door hinge brought him quickly around; he straightened, and at once forgot about the saddle.

Mary Quitman was just swinging the door shut behind her. She stood in the straw litter, looking at him; her face was pale, her eyes a dark stain in the lamplight, as she put a finger to her lips. "Uncle Abel's asleep," she whispered. "Dozed off in his chair about an hour ago."

"Oh."

When he didn't say anything else, she tried again. "Where —where were you?"

"Town," he said, and frowned. "Where else?"

"I—I just didn't know. After that scene at dinner . . ." She broke off. Yet there had been something in her voice and in her face that pulled him to a stand directly before her, frowning down into her eyes.

"Wait a minute! You never figured I'd taken off, did you? Run out on you, or something? Don't tell me that's what the old man thought!"

She nodded. "I'm afraid so." And then seemed to recoil from what she read in his eyes. "Joe, he—he carried on something awful! Said you'd shown your true colors, just like he'd always known you would. That you'd broken parole—probably gone hunting for Reb Beecher so you could join up with him again. Of course, *I* knew it wasn't true."

"Did you?" he retorted angrily. "I just bet! I bet you were half-believing it!"

"I told him he was wrong! I told him he didn't know you . . ."

Suddenly he was staring, dumfounded by an impossible thought. Under its prodding, he took another step toward her and almost lifted his hands to her shoulders. "Supposing he'd been right? Would it have mattered to you at all? Even a little?"

A frown creased the space between her brows. He thought her lip trembled. "Well, of course it matters! You know what it would mean if you jumped parole!"

"If I were going back to Reb Beecher," he reminded her harshly, "a broken parole would hardly make any difference! Mary . . ." Suddenly it had to be said. "These months, that I been working here for your uncle—they haven't been easy. Sometimes I've been of a mind where prison couldn't have been much worse! The old man—" He gave a shrug. "Well, he can't help the way he is, and the Lord knows I got every reason to be grateful to him! But still—"

She nodded, her eyes serious. "I know. You've taken a lot off of him. And until tonight you've never raised your voice."

"How could I—things being the way they are? I'm not complaining. Still, there's one thing—just about the only one—that's made it possible to take; and that was, being near you! You know I've never said anything," he went on blindly, blurting it out while her eyes seemed to grow larger and darker in the thin lantern light. "Never dared! After all, who am I to—?"

"Don't say that, Joe! You're good as anyone!" She laid a protesting hand on his arm.

Her touch did it. He knew he couldn't have held back. He'd been wanting her so long, and in the turmoil of feeling that lay on him just then her nearness struck down all defenses. Fumbling hands reached and dragged her to him. He must have taken her by complete surprise because she didn't fight—not even for the first long moment that his mouth found hers. Her lips were soft and he thought he felt them stir, responding to the kiss.

Then suddenly her hands were against his chest, pushing. He held her tighter and she moaned and wrenched her face away, and struggled with such surprising strength that he had to let her go. She nearly fell, stumbling out of his arms; she stared at him with a look almost of wild terror, the dark hair tumbling about her flushed face. And then she turned and fled; and long after the door swung shut behind her he stood where he was—shaking his head, completely baffled, and more than a little angry.

Was she afraid of him, or what? Surely she wouldn't deliberately lead a fellow on, work him up and then turn cold and push him away again! Not a girl like Mary Quitman! But, what was he supposed to do, or think? He flung up his arms and dropped them again. No point in a fellow who knew nothing at all about women, trying to understand her; just put it down as all of a piece with the way everything was going tonight. At any rate, he told himself grimly, he'd never put himself in a position again where she could repulse him. As far as she was concerned, from here on he spoke when he was spoken to. He would keep his distance—and if she didn't like it, let her figure out why!

26

The old roan tossed its head and shook the bridle, impatient and wondering why Joe didn't take it off so he could feed in comfort. "Sorry, old boy," Joe said, going to him and giving his neck a slap. "With you, at least, I know where I stand!"

And then he froze, as a rumor of nearing horses began to grow upon the stillness.

Not touching the bridle, he swung hastily to the lantern on the roof prop. He jacked up the chimney, plunged the barn into darkness with a breath. Then he crossed quickly to the door that Mary had used a moment earlier, and pressing himself close against the flimsy panel he cracked it cautiously open.

He had a good view of the yard, and the nearby sprawl of Quitman's sod house. There were four riders. They pulled their horses to a milling halt and the dust swirled and fell in tawny streaks, across the light of the window. One of the horsemen sang out: "Hello, the house!"

Joe Elliott knew that voice. It was the sheriff's; and something turned over inside him as he heard it. Sid Davis would only be here for one reason.

Now the door opened and Abel Quitman's tall, bearded shape appeared there. A moment later Mary came out behind him, carrying a lamp. By the muted glow it spread across the dust, Joe was able now to see the men who accompanied the sheriff. One was Tod Grandy. One was a Slaughter hand. But what really startled him was the white-haired figure whose solid bulk filled the other saddle.

This was Morgan Slaughter himself. Somehow it had never once occurred to him the most influential man in Union County would take it on himself to come personally on this errand. To Joe, it seemed like taking a mere barroom tiff pretty damned seriously.

Even at the distance Joe thought he could read the astonishment on Abel Quitman's bearded face. "In the name of Tophet! What's wrong? What brings you men here?"

It must not have even occurred to him to invite the group to light down or come into the house. And the sheriff didn't wait for such an invitation. "I'll make it short, Abel. Sorry to have to say it—but we want Joe Elliott."

Joe had to admit that old Quitman didn't appear too much surprised. He drew himself taller, while Mary, beside him, seemed to shrink a little. "You'll tell me what it is he's done, of course," the old man said stiffly. "Because, whatever it is, I have to share the responsibility. And it looks like it must have been something bad."

"Bad enough," Morgan Slaughter answered heavily. He was a good figure of a man, as solid in the saddle as years of range work could have made him—even though, in recent months, he'd been spending ever greater amounts of his time in the swivel chair of a bank president. He had a carrying voice that easily reached to the barn. "The charge is assault and robbery!"

Robbery! Joe Elliott shook his head in wordless protest. There was a mistake! What the hell was this man talking about?

And then he learned, with fast-increasing bewilderment. "I guess you know my son Rick, don't you? Well, he had himself a lucky streak at cards in Kallen's place in town this evening—tells me he picked up close to four hundred dollars. Elliott was right there in the bar, drinking, and saw him win it. And afterward—"

Slaughter was interrupted as Quitman asked something Joe couldn't hear. "No doubt of it at all," he answered curtly. "There are a couple dozen witnesses. Elliott picked a fight with Rick and beat him up pretty bad, before they could pull him off. Then he left; but he laid in wait outside. He jumped my boy. Knocked him out and took every cent he had on him!"

Joe found himself dazedly shaking his head as he heard out this incredible story. His hand was on the door, almost ready to push it open, when he caught himself.

Hold it! he thought. Don't be a damn' fool! Don't just walk out there!

The busy murmur of talk continued; but though he strained to listen, only an occasional word reached him now. Once he was sure he heard Mary's voice and he frowned, wondering what she could be saying—for shy Mary Quitman to speak up in front of these men, and at such a time, was an astonishing thing in itself.

Abel Quitman put an end to the discussion. "Far as I'm concerned," he declared loudly, "I wash my hands of him! I've thought many times it was a mistake, trying to make anything out of that Elliott; after this, I'm through! I don't think you'll find him here, though," he added. "It'd be my guess he's heading south, right now—straight for Indian Territory."

"I know he's not here," Joe heard Mary say hurriedly. "Only a few minutes ago—while Uncle Abel was asleep—I thought I heard something after the turkeys and I went outside with the shotgun. I looked into the barn and his roan was gone . . ."

"If it's all the same," Morgan Slaughter said, "I reckon we'll look around. Since we've ridden all this way."

Abel Quitman wasn't going to argue with Morgan Slaughter. "Sure—sure. Help yourselves," he said. "His bed's in the barn . . ."

CHAPTER V

The sheriff gave orders; the group began to dismount. But as they prepared to start their search, Joe Elliott was already going into belated motion.

Now he was glad he hadn't got around to unsaddling! The old roan didn't want to leave his stall again but Joe hauled him out, and to a small door at the barn's rear. The prairie was black and soundless. Still afoot, still leading the horse, Joe crossed wagon ruts and then headed straight north into its immensity, stumbling over the ground's irregularities in his hurry to get clear of this place and the imminent risk of discovery. It was a real temptation to throw himself onto the roan's back and kick him into a gallop, but that would have been fatal. Instead, he held himself under hard control; and when he had covered a hundred yards or so he halted, dropping low amid the sage so he could look back toward the farm and skyline any movement there.

Nothing stirred as yet, between him and the dark farm buildings.

Suddenly he realized his lungs were near the point of

bursting, and knew he had been holding his breath. He released it and then he straightened to his feet, convinced that he'd eluded his hunters—so far at any rate. One thing, he was grimly sure: No one was going to take him! No one was dragging him back to that town, to face a charge he hadn't a chance of licking. He didn't need to be told they'd throw him so deep into the pen, this time, he'd never see daylight. . . .

Leather popped as he lifted into the saddle. The old roan grunted a protest that was so loud he thought it must surely reach the ears of the men hunting him at the farm. He said, "Let's go, fellow!" and swung away at a walk, still pointing north.

When presently he paused to look back, the sod-house window was a fallen star lying on the prairie. Watching it, he heard a drum of hoofbeats start, then fade. The searchers had given up, he decided; they were going back without him. For the first time he began to breathe a little more easily.

Then all he could hear was the normal insect chorus, the sound of the wind over dry earth stubble. He turned, settling into the stirrups, and booted the old horse ahead.

But this wasn't the direction he wanted to go. As soon as he thought it was safe he changed course and started a wide circle, that gradually swung him around into the south again. The Quitman farm fell away, somewhere out of sight to his left. And presently he dropped into a country road cutting ahead of him, straight as a rule down the section lines—straight across the miles toward the Indian Nations.

There was a kind of homing instinct in that. A hundred miles south lay a haven for any man on the dodge, where he'd find no law to bother him except for a few Indian Police and a handful of overworked Federal marshals, spread far too thin. Joe Elliott had been in the Nations exactly once, but he remembered a place or two where Reb Beecher sometimes hung out. One, in particular, he thought he just might be able to find again.

There was a good piece of Kansas to travel first, though—on an old roan gelding that hadn't too many miles left. Joe had to discipline himself against using the spur on him. The old horse couldn't be treated that way; he went slogging on at a shambling gait, the best he had.

Now that there was time to think, Joe found himself wondering who it could have been that really slugged and robbed Rick Slaughter. Anyone in the saloon, he supposed, or who might have heard about the poker game. It could even have been the stock buyer, Lamb, taking a drastic means of recouping his losses. In any case, with the dark night to cover him he'd evidently done a good job; and now that the sheriff had seconded Morgan Slaughter's quick leap to the conclusion that Joe Elliott was the guilty party, it was hardly probable any real effort was going to be made to find out the truth.

Sheriff Sid Davis! he thought bitterly, remembering the pose of friendly concern for a young fellow trying to manage a fresh start against difficulties. All it took, apparently, was a word from Morgan Slaughter to bring him into line. After all, why bother looking for clues, when you had someone like Joe Elliott handy to pin it on—and someone as powerful as Slaughter to persuade you to see it that way?

Well, by God, they *didn't* have him! Not yet!

Sometime in the night he crossed the river—the Arkansas, wide and shallow and black as oil under the starlight. Later, and near exhaustion, he picked up the silhouette of an abandoned dugout. He'd been hoping for something like this. He approached cautiously, but it looked deserted all right.

Moving with an effort, he climbed down and stripped the saddle. Afterward he let the old horse graze awhile, as he sat and brooded with his back against the crumbling mud

32

wall of the dugout, watching the wheeling stars and listening to the chomp of the roan's jaws tearing at tough prairie grass. When he thought he could stay awake no longer he rose and gathered the trailing reins and led the horse, not without protest, down the steps. With the plank door propped across the opening, he felt safer. And there he slept, in warm darkness, amid the dust that was sent sifting down over him by rats that scampered in the grass roots overhead.

His dreams were far from easy. A time or two he found himself pawing awake with a stifled sense of being trapped and lost. But weariness had its way and at last even a buffalo stampede over the crumbling roof would scarcely have roused him. Next time he woke it was to find dust-swimming bars of sunlight probing the holes in the roof; he was startled to realize how late he'd let himself sleep.

There was nothing at all to eat. Joe shrugged as he pulled his belt up a notch and thumbed the prong. He lifted the door aside and cautiously put his head out but saw no one; he was glad now he'd thought to bring the roan inside. By daylight, the old horse would have been a signal, visible for miles. He led him up the steps, hastily saddled, and mounted.

He felt naked and exposed, riding on again under the glare of daylight. But he simply hadn't nerve enough to wait it out and do his traveling by night.

He kept pushing steadily, skirting wide of every farm and village he saw. He lost all sense of time, except for the slow crawl of the sun across the brassy sky, and the gnawing in his empty belly. Hard to judge the distance he covered, across that level, sunbrowned prairie; more and more frequently he found himself having to stop and let the old horse rest. And once, on climbing into the saddle, an ancient stirrup leather snapped and he had to make repair with a bit of haywire he fortunately found twisted in the harness.

Having no gun, he couldn't even knock over a jackrabbit. At last, hunger drove caution out of him. He picked a lonely looking place that reminded him a little of Quitman's—a sod house, with a dogtrot to separate the two rooms, and a brush-fence pen with a couple of horses running in it—and rode in through afternoon heat haze to ask for a handout.

He was met by a sour-looking man in overalls, who put a suspicious stare over the stranger, and his outfit, and then told him grudgingly he could light down but to keep damn' well away from the horses in the corral.

Joe Elliott had his uneasy meal, beans and salt pork and bitter coffee, sitting in the dirt with his back against a fence post, tin plate balanced on knee and the farmer's silent stare watching every bite he put away. That fellow would remember him, he thought as he rode on; damn' right he would. But having food in his belly was worth it. Besides, it couldn't be too many miles to the Border. If the old horse could only hold out, he actually began to think he might make it. . . .

Near sunset a couple of evenings later, Joe Elliott sore-footed down through a brushy ravine leading to the Canadian bottoms, deep inside the Cherokee Nation. A late sun slanted gold across the maze of brush and trees around him; insects danced in a hot stillness. Somewhere to the south the loops of the river gleamed beneath bluffs crowned with mahogany and oak.

He eased the heavy saddle down from his shoulder and straightened, hands at the small of his back, body worn and sweat-soaked inside his clothing. The wooded hills crowded around. Half-hidden in scrub, on a level bench above the ravine where he stood, a cabin reared its high-pitched shake roof and smoke spiraled from a mud chimney. Joe studied it a long moment, listening but hearing only the stillness of the deep woods.

He was some puzzled. He'd have expected to be challenged before this.

At the foot of a path that branched up from the ravine

trail toward the cabin on the bench, Joe saw a boxlike wooden frame and knew it must house a spring. Sight of it set the tight muscles of his throat to working as he picked up his saddle by the horn, to lug it the remaining distance. When he lifted the lid off the well boxing, the cool breath and rushing sound of the water greeted him. There was an iron dipper, and Joe scooped and drank gratefully; it tasted sweet and cold, better than what came from Abel Quitman's well.

Afterward, Joe sat on the ground and pulled off his right shoe. The heel of the sock was worn through and a blister had formed and broken. He winced as he gingerly examined it, trying to lap the frayed edges of cloth over the hurt. He was just pulling the laces tight again when the running hoofbeats of a pair of nearing horses brought him hurriedly to his feet.

The instincts of a fugitive put him in motion, almost before conscious thought registered the danger. He was in brush, squirming for better cover, as the riders drew rapidly nearer along the ravine trail. Hugging the earth, he looked back through a screen of leaves and branches and, just as the horsemen swept into view, saw his saddle lying on the ground, forgotten.

Too late then, of course. The sun spearing through the trees struck glints of brightness from harness metal, from guns in the holsters of the two riders, and from something pinned to the shirt of one of them. Even before he caught that, Joe had somehow been certain they were lawmen. Helpless, he watched and waited.

In his panic it seemed to him the saddle must be as unmistakable as a beacon; but then it came to him that they hadn't even noticed it. For they passed it by, turning straight up the trail to the cabin on the bench; and the moment they had cleared his hiding place he was out, darting forward and grabbing up the saddle and dragging it into cover with him.

He tossed it into the thickest brush; after that, a need to know what was happening at the cabin sent Joe Elliott scurrying up the rise. He kept low, staying in the shadows of the undergrowth, and getting in as close as he dared. A little breathless, he crouched and peered through a clump of leafy sumac.

The cabin was a crude log structure, facing south toward the river bottom, with a shake roof that dipped forward over a plank-floored porch. He saw a barn and sheds beyond, a horse pen with a good-looking black mare inside it, a few acres of tilled land with the timbered hills rising behind.

The riders had hauled rein in the dooryard clearing. Under the deep overhang of the porch roof he made out a figure standing in the doorway. It was a woman; Joe could see her long skirt, though her face was shadowed. But the bright tube of the shotgun in her hands was plain enough. Its muzzle slanted directly up at one of the mounted men, and the voice that came across the stillness was shrill with anger.

"Ain't no matter to me *whose* name you got on that warrant! Go ahead—search and be damned. But you best watch your step. You'll find nothin' here but a pair of defenseless women."

The man said something that failed to reach as far as Joe's hiding place. The woman's angry reply was even louder than before. "You heard what I said! And you can tell Ike Parker for me, I'm tired of him sending his deputies around to pester, every time they got a warrant. What do you think—that every penny-ante outlaw in the Nations spends his time at my place?"

"Belle," the one with the badge on his shirt said angrily, "you can't fool us by talkin' innocent! We know exactly what goes on around here. We know you and your husband, both, just got done spending a year in the pen for horsestealing."

"It was only nine months," she retorted hotly. "And we were framed."

"Oh, sure!"

The shotgun lifted; so did her voice. "Get out! This is my property—and I know my rights. You got no charge against anybody here. So you best ride before I really lose my temper!"

There was a moment when the scene hung fire, and the two men exchanged a look under the menacing eye of the shotgun. Then, with an abrupt gesture, the one who had done the talking swore and swung his bridles. His companion was close at his heels as he spurred back down the trail; quickly the rattle of hoofs faded and died.

And as silence returned, Joe Elliott let out a long breath that had been cramping his lungs. He supposed he was being too anxious. Little reason to think Morgan Slaughter's influence could reach this far from Union City, Kansas, and already have a bench warrant issued on him by Hangin' Judge Parker's Federal court over in Fort Smith. That might come later, of course; if the law found out he'd taken refuge in Indian Territory, Parker's manhunters might get the word to be on the lookout for him. But the machinery could scarcely be turning this fast. . . .

So, shaky with relief, Joe Elliott left his hiding place and worked back down the hill. He dug his saddle from the bushes and stepped out into the ravine trail, lugging it—and then turned with a start to see the woman standing less than a dozen paces away, waiting for him. This time, the shotgun was pointed straight at his own head.

"You can stand right where you are," she told him harshly.

CHAPTER VI

How in the world she'd managed to take him by surprise was past his imagining. Hastily he let the stock saddle drop to the ground at his feet. His glance tore away from the menacing eye of the gun muzzle, moved up the shining tube to the capable hands that held it with one finger hooked solidly around the trigger.

He swallowed. "Now, ma'am . . ."

"Guess you thought I never seen you, skulkin' there in them bushes," she said. "While I was getting rid of the John Laws."

Joe Elliott's eyes lifted from the gun, to the woman. She was well-built, of medium height, in the long skirt and the blouse with its sleeves rolled to the elbows and opened at the throat—a woman in her mid-thirties. But if the figure was good enough, the homely face that topped it held a compelling cruelty, in stabbing blue eyes and a mouth that closed like a trap. A wing of dark hair, sweeping across her forehead, shadowed the probing eyes.

"You don't appear to remember me," Joe Elliott said.

"Don't recollect ever layin' eyes on you."

"I'm Bart Dolan's kid brother. Name of Elliott. I come in here once with him and Reb Beecher."

"That's what *you* say."

"It's a fact, Miz Starr. You real sure you don't remember?"

The hard eyes made no concession. "I vaguely recall, now," Belle Starr told him curtly. "But that kid's in the pen. He was caught and sent up for the Emporia bank job."

"They let me out on parole; then I went and got in a little trouble and had to run for it. I was hoping to find Bart—and this place of yours seemed as likely as any."

"How am I supposed to know you're telling me the truth?"

"Look, Miz Starr! If I was lying—if I'd never been here before—how'd I of known the way? Younger's Bend ain't easy to find!"

"Judge Parker's boys seem to keep finding it," Belle commented dryly.

"Do I look like a Federal marshal? Look—I ain't even got a gun."

She surveyed him coldly, tallying the lack of one. She looked at the old saddle, beside him on the ground. "Ain't got a horse, either. How come? What happened to him?"

"He give out on me, a dozen miles back. I turned him loose. Wasn't much of a horse, to begin with, and I been pushing him hard. All the way from Kansas."

"What part of Kansas?"

"Union City. Know where it is?"

"Got some idea . . ." For the first time she seemed partially inclined to accept his story; for the first time, the shotgun muzzle eased slightly off its target. Suddenly she dropped the barrel onto her forearm so that it slanted at the ground. And though she could instantly swing it up again, Joe felt the cramping congestion inside his chest lessen a trifle.

"You look beat out," she said roughly. "If you're what you

39

say you are, looks like you may have had your trouble for nothin'. Because Dolan ain't here—nor Reb, either."

He had already guessed as much. "I just thought there was a chance they might be planning to meet here, after that railroad job. Or that you might happen to know where."

"If I did," Belle Starr snapped, "I ain't at all sure I'd tell you! I been called a lot of things. The newspapers call me 'the Bandit Queen' which is a lot of hogwash. But one thing I ain't is a big-mouth!"

"Yes, ma'am."

"I know a lot of the boys that hang out in the Nations. Some of 'em are good friends of mine. Time to time they drop around here at Younger's Bend for a meal or a night. But you don't keep friends by telling everything you know about 'em, to anybody that happens by. How long since you ate?" she added, the change of subject so abrupt it made him blink.

"Longer than I like to remember."

"Well . . . come up to the house. Pearl should have supper near ready. Now you're here, we may as well at least feed you."

"I'd sure appreciate it."

"Easiest way to keep an eye on you," she pointed out. "While I'm makin' up my mind." She motioned him ahead of her, with the muzzle of the shotgun. "Go on."

Acutely, spine-crawlingly aware of that gun, Joe grabbed his saddle and went limping up the path. He found himself listening for the swish of the woman's skirts behind him and the scrape of her footsteps, but she moved soundlessly. Perhaps she learned that from living among Indians the way she did, surrounded by the Starr clan. Their cabins were spotted all through these Canadian River bottoms, and it was something of a wonder he'd managed to avoid being picked up on his way in—maybe hauled up before murderous old Tom Starr himself.

He'd never seen Tom, but Bart had told him some things about the old clan chief, whom legend reported to have burned a whole family alive. He was Belle's father-in-law; by marrying into the tribe, she—a white woman—had earned a claim to these sixty-two acres of Indian land that her cabin sat on. Joe remembered meeting her husband, Sam—a tall, silent Cherokee with a look that could chill your blood.

The sun had almost gone, now, and its last light made a golden patina that smoothed over the primitive rawness of this place and gave a kind of wild beauty to the trees, the looping river, the shouldering hills. But it seemed an odd way for a white woman to live. Even a woman like Belle, who picked horse thieves for her friends and—so report had it—for her numerous lovers.

On instruction, Joe Elliott dumped his saddle on the porch and walked inside, ducking under the crude lintel and halting there. The cabin had only one room, with a packed clay floor and no other ceiling than the shakes and rafters of the roof. The furnishings—the table and chairs and two iron beds —were as crude as the rest of it. A girl turned from the stone fireplace with a steaming kettle she'd just taken off the crane. She stood holding it, looking the new arrival over. "Hey! Who's this, Maw?" she asked as Belle entered behind him.

Joe, fumbling off his hat, heard Belle's curt answer. "Nobody. Just a stray." She hung her shotgun up on a couple of wall pegs, and began rattling dishes onto the table. "He's eatin' with us."

Her daughter continued to regard the stranger with bold interest. "I'm Pearl," she said. "What's your name?"

"Joe Elliott." He felt vaguely irritated and uncomfortable under her steady gaze.

"You're a new one," she said, wagging her head. She'd be about eighteen, he supposed—full-bosomed and bare-legged in a sleazy cotton dress that looked too tight for her. And fairly pretty, in a brassy, round-cheeked way. Certainly he could see no resemblance to her hawk-faced mother, who was looking sharply from one to the other of the young pair now, with a hint of sour disapproval.

Pearl must have got her looks from her father, whoever he was; according to Bart, the outlaw Cole Younger, who was Jesse James's pal, seemed the most likely candidate. "If you ever seen Cole," Bart had told him once, "you couldn't doubt it—Pearl's the spittin' image of him. Him and Belle are supposed to have had an affair years ago, down in Texas. You'd think anybody'd be hard up, wanting anything to do with the old crow. But, maybe at eighteen she was easier to take."

"Does Belle claim Cole was the girl's paw?" Joe had asked.

"She's never bothered to deny it. Calls her Pearl Younger half the time. And would she go and name that place of hers Younger's Bend if there wasn't something behind the stories?"

Pearl wouldn't have been more than half-grown, at the time of Joe's previous sojourn at the Bend. At any rate, she hadn't been around then; and so this was his first look at Belle Starr's daughter. He was never at ease with strange girls, and there was something about this one that made him color a little, under her frank stare. He was dirty and he knew it; he could use a washing, and so could his shirt that had great dark circles of sweat showing under the arms. He worried the fingers of one hand through the tangle of his hair and shuffled his heavy farmer's shoes awkwardly on the clay floor. "Pleased to meet you," he mumbled.

"You come far?"

"A smart piece."

"Yeah, you look it!" She set the kettle down on the table, and with hand on hip gave him another glance that assayed the whole untidy length of him. Little as he knew about women, he had an untutored male instinct to the effect that modesty was a becoming asset in one. He compared this forthright Pearl Younger with quiet Mary Quitman, and keenly felt the contrast.

And then, thinking how remote the chances were he would ever see Mary again, he had to swallow down the choking sense of loss that went through him.

"Bet you're on the scout," Pearl said bluntly. "We don't often see any other kind but outlaws, around here. At that, you look better than some we get. How long will you be around?"

He opened his mouth to answer something vague, but Belle Starr spoke ahead of him. "Pearl!" she snapped, and her voice was sharp. "You never fetched up that water like I told you. Go do it."

The girl gave her mother a sour look. "Botheration, Maw!"

"You heard me."

"I can fetch it," Joe volunteered.

"The girl's no cripple. She'll do as she's told!"

Pearl shrugged, and picked up a bucket. Passing Joe on her way through the door, she deliberately let a shoulder brush against him and a bold eye slanted a look sideward into his. Then she was gone, at a leggy stride, swinging the bucket and whistling.

Joe turned to find Belle eying him with cold dislike; when she spoke, he knew why she had ordered Pearl out of the cabin. "I'll give you fair warning," she said, low and tight. "The same I give all the others. When you're around my daughter—you keep your hands to yourself!"

He could only stare like a fool. "Why, I never did nothing!"

"No—and I aim to see you don't! Hard enough to raise a good-lookin' girl out here without riffraff like you smellin' around, doin' all you can to get her into the brush. I'm gonna raise her respectable if I have to break her neck doing it!"

43

He didn't know what to say. Such talk sounded odd enough, coming from this uncouth woman with her raffish way of life and her shabby morals; but he supposed even Belle was enough of a mother to recognize, dimly, there was something better for a girl and want her child to have it. He said as earnestly as he could, "I told you the truth, Miz Starr. I come here hoping I could find news of my brother. That's all I want. I got no designs on your girl—you got to believe me."

Belle studied him closely. She shrugged. "I don't have to believe nothin'. Anyway, you're wasting your time. Maybe you ain't heard the whole story on that Santa Fe job."

Joe Elliott felt something cold touch his spine, like a finger. "I never heard a lot."

"Well, we get word of things, on the grapevine. Before I said anything, I wanted to be sure you're what you claimed you was—and, I guess you are."

A red light of sunset was fading, and the cabin was growing shadowy. As Joe waited, Belle went to a shelf and took down a kerosene lamp, put it on the table.

"Well?" he prompted her finally, unable to hold it back.

"Your friends got cut off," Belle told him bluntly as she removed the chimney of the lamp and prepared to light it. "They couldn't make it back toward the Nations. They had to swing north—and I reckon by now the whole State of Kansas is up in arms, to try and keep them from circling back." She struck a sulphur match, touched it to the wick. Yellow light leaped against the mud-daubed walls. Outside they could hear Pearl jauntily whistling her way up the path from the spring.

"You can stay the night," Belle said. "But no longer'n that. In the morning I want you gone. I got a notion Pearl's tooken sort of a fancy to you, and I don't need her gettin' interested in some punk kid. You hear me?"

"Yes, ma'am," Joe Elliott answered in a dead voice.

44

The clinking of the lamp's chimney into its brackets steadied the glow and drove back the shadows in the dingy cabin. Joe stared at the flame, but he saw nothing. His mind was stunned to a numbed vacancy, by what the woman had told him.

CHAPTER VII

It wasn't any sound, but the flare of lantern light washing across his sleeping face, that roused him. He lay a moment on his blanket, blinking at the glow, still drugged and dazed by sleep. The persistent glare finally worked through to him, then, so that he groaned and raised an arm across his eyes in protest.

With his eyes shaded he could see, suddenly, the legs of the man who held the lantern. They were encased in jackboots and shapeless butternut trousers. The barrel of a six-shooter gleamed faintly in the man's free hand—and suddenly Joe Elliott was wide awake.

He sat up abruptly, and the gun barrel lifted; but then the man let it fall back again. A voice said roughly, "So it *is* you!" The gun slid into its holster.

Night was black and silent, beyond the open door of the barn. Belle's black mare, Venus, stomped and snuffled in her stall.

"Take that damn' light out of my eyes!" Joe said irritably.

The man only grunted, but his arm lifted and as the lantern rose his face swam into the swaying circle of its yellow gleam.

It was a curious face, swart and ugly, the nose a mashed and flattened smear. Someone's boot must have done that to it. The jaw, shining with a stubble of wiry beard, worked rhythmically on a mouthful of cut plug.

Vince Choate turned his head and dropped a reeking gobbet of brown juice into the straw. He said, "The old bitch told me she had Joe Elliott bedded down out here—or somebody claiming to be him. Hell, boy! I was thinkin' you'd still be in Lansing."

Of all Reb Beecher's gang, Joe had liked Choate the least. He was a bigger, tougher Tod Grandy—hard of hand, foul of mouth, a man who had treated him with contemptuous dislike. But here at least was one of the gang—alive and in the flesh, and escaped from the tightening net of Kansas law. Joe Elliott was brought quickly to his feet.

"Vince!" he exclaimed. "I heard you were in trouble after that train job—that the law had cut you off. But you got through! Where are the rest? They here with you?"

The other looked at him, through a long and silent moment. Then he laughed sourly, without a trace of humor. "Oh, hell! We got through in great shape! Luke Miles is dead. Jim Ordway's in the house so bad shot up I don't know how I got him this far . . ."

Now for the first time Joe could see clearly the fatigue that rode this man. His face and clothing were filthy with trail dust. He carried the reek of horse sweat. His eyes were rimmed with red, his cheeks shadowed. Joe forced out the question: "Where's Bart?"

Choate lifted heavy shoulders. "God damned if I know! Him or Reb, either. Last I saw of them, was in a patch of woods a few miles south of Newton, with a sheriff's posse all around it.

"That's when we split. After Jim and me got away, we heard some shooting but there was no damn' use at all, going back."

Joe Elliott stared. "You telling me you run out on them?"

"I'm tellin' you, it was every man for himself!" The eyes narrowed thoughtfully. "Belle says you're on the scout, yourself. Thinks you got the notion of tryin' to join up with us." He snorted. "All I can say is, you picked a great time! The gang's run into bad luck before—but this is once when we were really shot to pieces!"

He turned away, then, light from the lantern swinging and bobbing around him. In the doorway he paused, looking back. "There's a couple horses out there, both dead beat. Take care of 'em."

Normally, Joe Elliott might have taken exception to this way of being ordered around. But now, in a daze, he said merely, "Sure, Vince." And after that Choate was gone, taking the lantern with him.

Joe had gone to bed fully dressed except for his shoes. He sat down and hastily pulled them on, wincing at the pain of his blistered heel. Afterward, he hurried outside.

The pattern of stars was out big, and the night so still he thought he could hear the river lapping, yonder, under the bluff to the south. The cabin windows glowed with lamplight, and as he hobbled up from the barn he saw the horses standing with drooping heads, tied to the corner post of the porch. One was a gray, one a buckskin. Their flanks gleamed wetly in the windowglow; Joe's palm found the slickness of sweat.

He flipped the reins free of the post and was about to lead both animals away when he heard a smothered giggle in the porch shadows. Two figures broke apart there, to be silhouetted against the open door—Vince Choate and Pearl. Even as Joe watched, without really meaning to, he saw Vince pull the girl roughly back and the shadows become one again, briefly. Then Pearl broke away and through the door, but she glanced back and her face was laughing. The man, too, was grinning as he swaggered into the cabin after her.

Joe Elliott shrugged. Belle had a job on her hands, it looked like, if she expected her daughter to follow her precepts rather than her example. . . .

In the barn, by lantern light, he busied himself with unsaddling the horses, letting his hands do the work while his mind digested the news Choate had brought with him. He tried to tell himself that he still knew nothing definitely bad —that two seasoned campaigners like Bart and Reb Beecher could beat out a posse if any man could. But somewhere, behind his eyes, he could see that patch of woods Vince had described to him—the fugitives scrounging for their lives as the ring of hunters tightened. He could almost hear the banging of guns, watch the dusty leaves clipped free by searching bullets and drifting down through patches of light and shade.

The horses were badly used, and one was so soaked with blood that he searched carefully for the mark of a bullet but couldn't find any. It must be Jim Ordway's blood, then. The saddle was sticky with it. As he cleaned it up as best he could, Joe wondered how a man so wounded could still be alive.

He blew the lantern and went up to the cabin again.

Night was far spent and there was a faint rumor of dawn above the eastern ridges. The lamp in the cabin still burned. As he limped toward it, favoring the blister, there was a sudden bubbling, tearing scream that ended in a falling groan and left him hauled up in midstride with his heart thumping, the short hairs bristling on his neck. Then he was in the doorway, and he saw the hurt man lying limp and unconscious on one of the iron beds, and the three people standing over him looking at something Belle Starr held on the palm of one bloody hand. "Carrying a thing like that in him," she said gruffly, "it's a pure wonder he ain't dead long since!"

She grimaced and flung the bullet into the fireplace. After that she dropped the knife she'd dug it out with onto the table, washed her hands in a basin and dried them on a towel

49

Pearl handed her. Vince Choate, meanwhile, had resumed his seat which he'd left briefly for the purpose of holding Jim Ordway down, until the shock of the knife's probing finally knocked him out. Vince had been interrupted in the midst of a hurried meal and now he returned to it, heartily wolfing the food like a man half-starved and not at all perturbed by the bloody basin at his elbow, or by any concern over his friend's condition.

On the doorsill, Joe Elliott stared at the hurt man. Ordway lay on his back, breathing harshly through his mouth. The unshaven face, that Joe remembered, had a drained and waxen look about it. He knew then that Jim Ordway was dying; but the man was fighting for every inch.

Belle ripped cloth with an explosive sound, as she prepared to bind the gaping chest wound. Vince Choate, looking up, caught sight of Joe Elliott and he said loudly, "Get them horses tended to, kid?"

Joe nodded without answering. He came into the room and took a chair at the table. There was an empty mug in front of him; without being asked, Pearl filled it from the big graniteware coffee pot. He watched the dark liquid swirl into the cup and watched the steam rise as the pungent tang of it hit his nostrils; but food of any kind was the last thing he was interested in just then and he let it sit untouched.

"That's that!" Belle grunted, her job done. She caught Pearl's eye, with a jerk of her head and an order to clean up the mess; and as the girl moved sullenly to obey, her mother came over to the table. Vince Choate, pushing back his plate, ran a sleeve across his mouth and returned her hostile stare.

"You've already heard," she said, "what I think about you bringing anybody here in that shape and dumping him on me!"

"No place else to take him."

"Well, you can take him away again. First thing when he's able."

Joe Elliott blurted indignantly, "He can't be moved, and you know it!"

The cruel eyes turned to him, rested on his face for a considerable moment. Then she swung back to Vince Choate. "I'm telling you now, if you should go and bring the law in here—"

He shrugged. "Hell! Will you quit grousing? Nobody yet ever brung nothin' to Younger's Bend that you couldn't handle!"

Joe watched the anger shape Belle's mouth. He saw the knuckles of the hand that was in his range of vision clench white, and thought for a moment that she was going to strike Choate in the face. The outlaw stiffened as though he had the same thought. Across the room Pearl Younger stood motionless, staring.

She knew her mother's moods. She must have witnessed violent scenes far beyond any a person that young was equipped to absorb. Suddenly Joe couldn't help feeling a little sorry for her.

He got up and walked out of there.

Dawn was just breaking on Younger's Bend. High overhead a string of tiny clouds glowed with the color of Jim Ordway's spilled blood, and he could see them reflected in the misting coils of the river. Nothing moved. In this golden morning, with the slow spiral of smoke from the cabin chimney and the tap of a woodpecker higher along the timbered ridge, it seemed there'd never be a more peaceful world than the one he looked upon.

Yet its rugged beauty was lost on Joe Elliott. He'd never have thought he could be homesick for the miserable soddy on Quitman's quarter section, but just now it seemed in memory a haven of security. Standing there on that hillside in the Cherokee Nation, thinking of Mary and of Bart being hounded somewhere by his enemies, he was suddenly the loneliest man in the world.

CHAPTER VIII

It took Jim Ordway one more whole day to make it. It seemed incredible he could clutch the fraying thread of life so long—never once regaining consciousness. As he lay there in the bed, the horrible rasp of his breathing took over all other sounds and filled his hearers with something like impatience for him to get his dying over with.

And then, just at noon, the breathing stopped.

There was no ceremony in his passing, and—so it seemed to Joe Elliott—damned little human feeling. Belle declared she wanted him removed from the bed and the cabin as soon as possible; there wasn't room enough for the living, let alone the impersonal dead she hadn't wanted there in the first place. Joe volunteered to dig the grave, and with Belle's grudging consent picked a spot far back under the ridge behind the cabin, where he didn't think Jim Ordway would be disturbed.

It seemed about as nice a place as a man could ask to be buried, if he had to die among strangers and far from home. There was brush and some big rocks and a few trees, and he sank the spade bit under the branches of a big old persimmon, finding it good to be doing physical work again. Anything, to help work off some of the morbid thoughts a fellow couldn't escape at such a time—thoughts about his own future, and what his end would be and who, if anybody, would be around to bother or care when it happened.

Lacking a coffin, they simply wrapped Jim Ordway in his own saddle blanket, and Joe and Vince Choate toted him to his final resting place. Neither Belle nor her daughter joined them—they were already busy cleaning the last traces of the dead man out of the cabin; and Belle had begun hinting broadly that, with him gone, the other two were welcome to pull out any time as far as she was concerned.

Even though there'd been no hint of any deputy marshal following Vince Choate into the Bend, neither was there sign of the remaining members of the gang. But so far Vince showed no inclination of being ready to leave.

Joe had the task of filling up the grave, and it wasn't too pleasant hearing the first clods fall onto the blanket-covered bundle. Working alone he finished the job, rounding off the heap of fresh-turned earth with the flat of the spade. Then he took up the piece of shingle he'd chosen for the purpose, got out his knife and dug open the blade.

The letters he carved were crude but he dug them deep, to make them last—Jim's name, and the date. And that was really all he knew. Probably no one could have told where the man came from, or even his age. Joe set the board at the head of the mound, drove it deep with blows of the spade and braced it with stones. Afterward he sleeved sweat from his face, pulled his hat on, and walked back to the cabin.

He was working at the woodpile an hour later, splitting kindling and listening to the echoes bounce off the neighboring ridges, when he saw the single horseman approaching on the river trail. Joe dropped the ax, glancing around quickly. He was all by himself just then—Vince wasn't in evidence, or either of the women. He thought of the shotgun on its nails in the cabin, but for some reason didn't move to get it. Instead he stood where he was, alert and watchful. The horseman came slowly up the hill through sunlight and silent leaf shadow; it was Reb Beecher.

Reb Beecher—*alone!*

For a man whose tenure on life had depended so many years on constant vigilance in outsmarting and outtricking his enemies, he seemed strangely unwary. He rode straight ahead, letting the horse set its own gait—like a man either too weary or too careless to bother where he went. Joe, watching, had a chance for a good long look at the outlaw.

He'd remembered a battle-scarred gray wolf of a man, indomitable and fierce, with a fanaticism for a long-lost cause that was oddly like the intolerant religious zeal of Abel Quitman. But the man who rode up the hill toward him now was slump-shouldered, weary in every line; when at last he reined his horse and lifted his head for a look around the clearing, Joe saw a face that had sagged and aged more than would have seemed possible, three short years ago.

He stood without speaking, waiting to see what the man would do. Reb Beecher pulled himself up as though with an effort, preparing to dismount. Then, with a booted foot lifted from stirrup, he suddenly noticed the figure standing silent by the woodpile. The old outlaw froze, and a hand touched the holster he wore strapped to his leg. But the holster was empty, a fact he seemed to have forgotten. He let the hand fall away again, while he squinted narrowly.

"It's all right, Mr. Beecher," Joe said. "There's nothing to be afraid of. Vince Choate's here, and we been watching for you."

"Vince? He made it, then?"

Joe nodded. "Jim Ordway's dead. We buried him this morning."

He didn't want to ask but he had to: "What about Bart?"

The old man didn't seem to have heard. He was looking at Joe, in scowling perplexity. "I don't know you!"

Quickly Joe introduced himself.

Straggling brows drew down until the squinting eyes became almost invisible. There was nothing to indicate what the outlaw was thinking; but he didn't question any further. Instead, he threw a leg across the saddle and stepped heavily down, a stocky figure in shabby denims and run-over boots. He stood inches short of the impression Joe's memory had built of him.

"Is Belle here?"

"Should be. I don't see her at the moment, though."

Beecher ran the ball of a thumb across his mouth. "Wonder if she'd have anything to eat, there in the house? My belly's caved. Lost track of time, and meals, and everything else!"

"Come on in," Joe Elliott said gruffly. "We'll see if we can scrape something together."

The horse wasn't in too bad shape. They left it standing under the saddle and went inside, where Reb Beecher flopped with a groan into one of the crude homemade chairs, dropped his flat-crowned hat onto the floor beside him, and scrubbed a stubby-fingered hand through woolly, iron-gray hair. He seemed to be taking it for granted Joe would wait on him; and after a moment's hesitation the young fellow shrugged and turned to see what he could find on the shelves.

There was a slab of cold meat, some pone, and coffee that had been boiled so long that it poured thick and black into the cup. Beecher gulped it down neat, not bothering with the jar of molasses—"long sweetenin'"—Joe set out for his use. Then he tackled the cold roast, hacking off big chunks and wolfing it down as though he hadn't eaten in a week. Joe Elliott, forking a chair with his arms folded upon its back, watched him in mingled distaste and pity.

55

He said finally, "I done asked you once and you never answered me. What about Bart?"

The busy jaw stilled, with one whiskered cheek distended over a bulging chaw of meat. The red-rimmed eyes peered sharply at Joe. "What about him?"

"I want to know where he is!" Joe managed to keep an edge on his patience. "Vince said you stayed together when the bunch split up, south of Newton. And then what happened?"

The old outlaw's mouth drew down, hard. "What happened?" he repeated. "Ain't that what I been askin' myself, ever since we hit that train!" He shook his head, with the air of a man bewildered by the blind twistings of fate. "Never seen so many blue coats since the day me and Quantrill run into that detachment of 'em at Lone Jack, in Missouri, back in Sixty-two. That time, we had the Youngers with us. In them days we could of took them Yankee sojers and took 'em proper . . ."

Joe Elliott gritted his teeth. The old man's wild, fanatic eyes were gleaming, his ashen cheeks beginning to take color as he called up the ghosts of a vanished day. It had taken almost nothing to set him off, which must surely be a bad sign. The great days of guerrilla warfare meant more to him than the grim realities of the present.

"You were gonna tell me about Bart," Joe prompted him, trying to ease him back onto the track. "Where did you leave him?" He felt his temper going. It suddenly didn't matter that this man was Reb Beecher, whose very name had been enough once to strike terror. "Damn it!" he gritted. "Do you hear what I'm sayin' to you?"

That brought him the old man's stare, flaring with a glitter that nearly put him in his place. "Be careful how you talk, boy!"

"I'll talk as I damn please! I ain't afraid of you. I want an answer: *Where's Bart?*"

A moment longer the fanatic eyes gleamed at him; then it was as though tiredness turned out the lamp behind them. Old Reb's shoulders hunched and he shoved another slab of corn pone into his mouth. "Dunno where he is," he said shortly. "Hard to say where they might of took him to."

"*Took* him?" Joe grabbed the back of the chair with both hands, tightening on it until they started to ache. "You ain't sayin'—he's been captured?"

"It's what I'm tryin' to tell you, ain't it?" Beecher kept chewing and swallowing, and washing it down with the vile coffee. His words came alternately clear and muffled by his eating.

"They jumped us in a crick bottom, just coming on dusk. That was some time after we'd went and lost our hosses. We was dead beat—takin' turns tryin' to steal a few winks whilst we could. I never heard or seen a thing—never had time to sing out—"

"What are you tellin' me?" Joe Elliott cut in, in a tone of ice. "Was it your turn on guard? You went to sleep, maybe —let 'em close in while Bart was counting on you for warning . . ."

Reb's scowl was thunderous, but he couldn't keep the truth from showing through. "We was both dead beat, I tell you!" he lashed back, his voice rising. "And then all hell busted loose! A man couldn't even think straight. I got into the brush somehow, and when I looked around for Bart the whole pack was closin' in on him. He put up a good fight, too. But his gun was empty, and I'd lost mine. Couldn't of done a thing to help."

"So you just crawled away," Joe finished, in a tight throat. "Saved your own hide, and left him to face a mob!" He drew a long breath. "What the hell you reckon they did with him?"

"Well, they never shot him anyway." This time Beecher didn't rise to the contempt in the other's voice. Perhaps he was too exhausted; or perhaps his own conscience didn't give

57

him the heart. "I heard nary a gun fired. Don't suppose he could of fought 'em for long—they was too many. Damn it, boy, I'd of gone back if I'd thought—"

"Reckon I've heard all I need to!" said Joe abruptly, as he hitched up off his chair. The old outlaw bridled.

"Now, listen here! I ain't gonna have no kid tell me—!"

"Aw, shut up!"

He stumbled outside, blinded by what he'd heard. He set a shoulder against a post holding up the porch roof and leaned there, staring at the played-out horse Reb Beecher must have stolen somewhere in his long flight back to the Nations.

Well, he supposed he had his answer. If Bart wasn't swinging from a tree—victim of an overzealous bunch of men who didn't know the difference between a sheriff's posse and a lynch mob—then he was probably sitting in a cell in some small-town Kansas jail right now, waiting for the law to have its way with him. Joe knew those cells—he'd spent his share of time in them, before and during the trial that sent him up to Lansing. He knew the steel bunks, the sleazy blankets and the lice, the disgusting food, the stench of sweating bodies and of the slop bucket that never got emptied half often enough.

Beecher hadn't really been able to tell him much for certain; for all he knew to the contrary, Bart could have been hurt in the capture. Wherever he was, whatever shape he was in, he'd be alone—helpless in the hands of his enemies.

Just then an outbreak of shouting jarred him. Joe Elliott shook loose of his dreary thoughts, recognizing Belle Starr's shrill voice and the bass rumbling of Vince Choate. They sounded—he thought as he hastily quit his post—as though they came from the barn. Sure enough, rounding the cabin's corner he saw the barn door burst open and Pearl came running wildly into the open. She looked sadly disheveled, her hair streaming and loose straw clinging to it. Her mother appeared, a step behind her.

Belle's face was contorted in rage; she had a bullwhip coiled in one hand. She grabbed Pearl's arm and at once the girl fell to fighting, clawing at the hand that held her prisoner, and both of them screaming like banshees. Then Pearl broke free. She stumbled and went down in a sprawl of bare and shapely legs.

Belle shouted, "You little bitch! Ain't I tried to raise you decent? I'll cut the hide off you!" The lash in her hand shook out, circled and struck; and Pearl screamed in pain and terror.

Vince Choate had come lurching out of the barn. His shirt was unbuttoned and he was tugging clumsily at the belt of his trousers. Cursing, he lunged at Belle but she eluded him, whirling as she stepped away. The whip circled and darted again and this time the lash took Vince squarely across the face. He roared and fell back as a streak of blood sprang out. Belle's arm rose, trailing the leather, and the outlaw flung both arms across his face, in full retreat before her.

"I'll show you!" she screeched. "Carry on behind *my* back!"

Belle swung again and started once more for her daughter. Pearl, huddled on the ground, cringed and whimpered hysterically, "Maw! No, Maw—*please!*"

Eyes glittering, Belle set her feet and again the whip started to rise. But by then Joe had reached her and he grabbed it. Belle turned on him, hissing like a snake as she tried to wrest it from his hand. Spittle stung his cheek. Grimly he fought with her. He trapped her arms, managed to jerk the whip away from her. Quickly he flung it over the fence into the horse pen.

"Now, cut it out!" he shouted; and there must have been something sobering in his look and his voice. Belle stared at him, her breast lifting and falling as she gasped for breath. But she had stopped her raging.

He looked around, in a suddenly renewed silence. Pearl had got to her knees and was sobbing and rubbing her shoulder. Vince Choate stood with the blood running down his cheek. And now Joe saw even Reb Beecher had come from the house to watch what was going on.

Joe Elliott was in no mood to remember that, in all their eyes, he was little more than a fresh kid. "Is this the only thing you got to do?" he demanded, turning on Vince. "With the dirt not even settled on Jim Ordway's grave? And Bart setting in a jail up in Kansas?"

Vince's scowl was fierce, but he was on the defensive. "What I do or don't do ain't gonna mean anything to Jim," he retorted. "And far as Bart's concerned—" Then he broke off, for he too had caught sight of Reb Beecher. "Reb! Hey! When'd you turn up?"

"I ran into the boy," Reb told him. "He was fixing me something to eat."

"Oh, he was?" Belle gave a snort. "Well, now, wasn't that generous of him!" she said, with fine sarcasm. "Don't know what any of you are doin' here, in the first place. Nobody invited you." She looked at her daughter, who was on her feet now. Pearl's face and her clothing were fouled with dirt and streaked with blood from the cuts of the bullwhip. "And ain't *you* a fine sight! Go on—you get in the house!" When Pearl didn't move Belle raised her fist and the girl sidled hurriedly closer to Joe Elliott, as though expecting him to protect her.

He wasn't of a mood to.

"Did they really get Bart?" Vince Choate asked, and hearing Beecher's affirmative growl he made a gesture that was little better than a shrug. "Tough. We're just lucky it wasn't either of us!"

Suddenly, disgust was very nearly a physical illness in Joe Elliott. He could smell its sour scent, feel it as an upward pressure in his throat that he had to swallow convulsively to hold down. "It didn't happen to you," he said, in a choked voice that drew their eyes to him, "so it's all right that it

60

happened to Bart or to Jim Ordway! And after all the years you rode together!" His mouth twisted in revulsion. "Reckon I'd be shamed to admit to such thinkin'!"

"And just what would you say we do about it?" Vince challenged.

"We could maybe find out where Bart is," he answered. "And then, by God, we could see about springing him!"

Belle Starr said flatly, "You'd never stand a chance!"

"A better chance than if we wait till they've put him away in Lansing—where we'd never hope to get at him!"

Vince looked at Reb Beecher, with a sneer. "Reb, this kid must be plain crazy."

"Rather be crazy my way, than sane like you!" He turned on the leader. "What about it? Anybody here got the guts to try?" He seemed forgetful who was the chief here, and which the young fellow who'd simply walked in uninvited.

A scowl darkened Reb Beecher's trail-grimed face. "It's out of the question!" he said flatly, shaking his head. "No point in all of us gettin' killed for nothin'."

"If *you* want to tackle it, kid," Vince Choate put in, "go right ahead. You're plenty welcome!"

"And maybe I will!" Joe Elliott retorted.

"All by yourself?"

The big man's scornful laughter snapped the last threads of patience—and, perhaps, of common sense. Even for the whole gang, the idea was unreasonable, as Vince and Reb both had the wits to see. But common sense wasn't Joe Elliott's long suit, he guessed. Without another word of argument, he turned and walked with a purposeful stride into the barn.

He had just finished cinching his old saddle on the buckskin when Vince Choate entered. The outlaw, seeing what he was up to, let out a bellow. "Where the hell you think you're going with my hoss?"

"I'm borrowin' him," Joe answered, and stepped smoothly

into the saddle. "You can get him back when and if I see you again."

"You pile offa there!"

Roaring, Vince started toward him. The horse tossed its head and backed nervously; but Joe's hand was steady and determined on the reins and now, from behind his belt, he dragged out a six-shooter.

"Hey! And my gun!"

Vince Choate glanced at the nail where he'd left it hanging for convenience while he dallied with Pearl. "I'm borrowin' this, too," Joe told him. And as Vince started to charge, he worked the trigger.

Concussion shook the walls; muzzle flash smeared the barn's shadows. A warning bullet chewed into dirt and straw in front of the outlaw's boots and brought him up with a yell. And Joe kicked the buckskin forward.

Vince Choate sprang aside; he rode straight past the man, ducking as he cleared the open doorway. There was no one in the yard. Giving the buckskin his head, Joe went pounding past the cabin, into the downward trail leading to the river.

Once he looked back, as Belle Starr came hurrying out to stand in the dooryard staring after him, an arm raised to shade her eyes. She was still standing there when the twisting of the trail pulled a screen of trees and brush between, and Younger's Bend was lost behind him.

CHAPTER IX

Flint Rock, Kansas, was a smear of gray dust and gray buildings that seemed to swim in the blast of noonday heat. The smell of dust and blistering paint rose from it, and the tired sounds of a land half-smothered by August—the rasp of paper-dry leaves in the cottonwoods overhead, the snapping of grasshoppers in weeds that choked the roadside ditches.

When Joe Elliott dismounted and tied the buckskin to a tree branch he knew he had ridden too long and too hard under that punishing sun. His shirt was scalding sweat; he felt dehydrated. He took a moment to fiddle with a split seam in the saddle leather, letting his stare roam the town while his horse lowered its head to hunt for a bit of grass. The core of the village was this single crossroads, where a straggling street cut the main wagon road. Even here, almost no life stirred. A lone saddle horse drooped, disconsolate, its neck thrust beneath the thin shade of a tie pole. A cur dog wandered across the dust and plopped down exhaustedly in front of a door.

A couple of town kids came trotting along the path toward Joe, rattling sticks over the palings of a picket fence. Suddenly one halted. "Hey!" he exclaimed, pointing across the road. "I seen him just then! Right there in the window. I got a good look!"

The other challenged. "Aw, you never either! You sure it was him?"

"Couldn't be anybody else. He's the only prisoner right now, ain't he?"

"I still don't think you seen him," the second boy muttered in dark jealousy.

They stood peering over the shimmering street, hard and brown and knobby-spined in their overalls. Joe Elliott hadn't failed to spot the stone jail building, yonder, that appeared hardly bigger than a good-sized icehouse. It normally would be used as a drunk tank, a storage place for occasional disturbers of the peace. He cleared his dry throat.

"Who is it you boys are talking about?"

They gave him a look. The first kid said, "It's Bart Dolan, mister! You heard of Bart Dolan, I reckon!"

"I reckon," he agreed carefully.

"He's a-sittin' right in that jail! My paw says they'll hang him sure, when they figure it's safe to move him to the county seat."

Joe felt his heart slog out a hurried beat. He asked, too quickly, "What's the matter? Why can't they move him?"

"Don't you know *nothin'*, mister? Because he got shot, that's why—when the posse jumped him, after that train holdup. This was the closest so they fetched him here. Everybody thought sure he was gonna die."

The second boy said, "Guess they won't be leaving him here much longer."

"Who says? Doc Ramsey himself told my paw, it'll be another week before he's well enough."

"Oh, yeah? Then what's the sheriff from Newton doing in town? Why'd he go and bring a wagon and a couple of deputies with him? Didn't we just see 'em with ol' Dobbs, in the eat shack?"

"Who's Dobbs?" Joe Elliott asked.

"Town marshal, of course." The boy's tone scoffed at such ignorance. "I bet he's gonna be glad to get Bart Dolan off his hands! Betcha old Bart's killed more'n a hundred men. More'n Jesse James, even."

"Aw, I bet he ain't!" the other boy retorted, and they were off again in the shrill aggressive argument of boyhood. The stranger was forgotten.

He already knew most of what they'd just told him. Scarcely had he crossed the Kansas border than he began to pick up rumors that Bart Dolan was being held in jail at Flint Rock; one thing he hadn't heard, the thing that alarmed him now, was that about Bart being wounded. All along, Joe had been accepting Reb Beecher's assurance that there'd been no more gunfire after he weaseled out of the trap and left Bart Dolan to face the enemy alone. Obviously, Reb was mistaken.

Now, in alarm, Joe Elliott could see that if Bart was as bad hurt as these kids had told him, it would double the size of a job that had already looked tough enough.

He took a deep breath and stood staring at the stone building—gauging the strength of the strap-iron bars on the window and on the iron-enforced slab door, hoping he might possibly catch a glimpse of Bart. He was even tempted, for a moment, to go over there and try to speak to his brother through the window, but he quickly discarded that idea. It could make him entirely too conspicuous.

He turned and looked back along the street, to where he could see the word *EATS*, in big letters, on a wooden signboard jutting out from the line of building fronts. As he considered it, one hand moved to touch the reassuring hardness of the gunbutt he'd shoved behind his waistband, under the shirt. He hoped it didn't make too plain a bulge. He knew he didn't look like much—dirty and sweaty, and beginning to show his need of a shave. Yet he could think of only one way in which he might learn more he needed to know. Before he could lose his nerve, he turned and walked along the pathway, beside the weed-choked stretch of picket fence, and stepped up onto the end of the high plank walk.

The eat-shack window was none too clean, but despite a smear of noon sunlight on the glass he could make out four men seated at the counter. A rumbling drift of man-talk reached him. It stopped abruptly as Joe Elliott pulled the screen door open and walked inside.

He nearly backed out again. Cooking odors and a withering blast engulfed him. A beefy cook, in undershirt and apron, was frying eggs in a skillet; every explosion of popping grease seemed almost to hit him in the face. In a sudden silence, the newcomer stood and felt himself probed by staring eyes. He knew he couldn't retreat now. He let the screen door go shut behind him, as he looked the place over, and then made for an empty stool farther along the counter.

"Kid!"

Joe halted, stiffening. For one bad moment he knew an irrational conviction that he'd been recognized—that Sheriff Sid Davis, or maybe old man Slaughter, had had foresight to warn the authorities in Flint Rock they had better be watching for Bart Dolan's half brother, a kid on the prod who just might have it in his head to try some fool play. Well, he would simply have to brazen it out. He turned slowly, face carefully expressionless, fingers toying with an unfastened shirt button just above the handle of that hidden gun.

"You ain't from around here, are you?"

Even lacking a badge, Joe could have guessed which of these was the sheriff from Newton—the chunky, tough-looking fellow with the heavy brows, and the cheeks raddled by old pockmarks, had "lawman" scrawled all over him. His two deputies were a nondescript pair. Town Marshal Dobbs, then, would be the stoop-shouldered old man whose bony skull showed through a thatch of thinning, graying hair; and this was the one who had spoken.

Knowing that, even needing a shave, he had a face that looked considerably younger than his years, Joe decided to take the cue from the marshal's question. He made himself sound as simple as possible. "Huh?"

The marshal scowled impatiently. "I said, I don't remember seeing you before."

Joe blinked and scratched himself under one arm. "Naw, I'm from down to Coffeyville. We ain't had it so good this summer. Hoppers got our corn, and Paw, he's been laid up pretty bad. Thought I'd come north and try to do some harvestin'. They need any harvest hands around Flint Rock?"

The old fellow scowled at him. "Not in August. I think you'd know that."

"Well, I knowed 'twas so, down in Coffeyville. I thought it might be different up north here."

"Up north? Hell, you're only some fifty miles from home!"

"Yes sir. Farthest I ever been."

One of the deputies loosed a snort of scornful laughter. The marshal made a dismissing gesture with one hand. "You better go back there, kid. Or you could try the wheat fields, on up toward Dakota. Ain't apt to be nothing around here for you."

"Yes sir. Thanks."

He attempted to look disappointed but he felt mainly relief as, accepting the tale, Marshal Dobbs turned back to his companions.

Joe climbed onto a stool and spoke to the cook, who was scowling as he wiped big hands on the front of a sweaty undershirt. "Coffee. And a sinker." Wordlessly the man slopped black coffee into a mug and set it in front of him, dropped a spoon beside his saucer, and followed both with a doughnut on a plate. He scooped Joe's money into a cash drawer under the counter, and after that went back to working at the stove.

Joe Elliott's stomach was tight with tension and didn't actually want the food, but he made himself sip at the coffee while, from under his hatbrim, he studied the lawmen down-counter from him. He felt he'd blunted any suspicion, yet he soon saw that his entrance had put a damper on the talk he'd interrupted. It didn't take up again. He hardly knew what he'd hoped to learn; but now this stretching silence, broken only by sounds of eating and the tick of a clock on a shelf behind the counter, began to work at his nerves. He began to tell himself he'd taken a bad risk for nothing.

Then the marshal, pushing back an empty plate, got to his feet. He said to the man behind the counter, "Ain't that grub ready yet?"

"Coming up."

The cook took the skillet off the fire, flipped the eggs onto a plate and set this on a tray, together with a mug of coffee and some slabs of bread. He clattered silverware after them, spread a cloth over the whole and set it on the counter. By now the other lawmen had finished their meals and were standing around, working with toothpicks they'd taken from a waterglass full of them. "There you are," the cook grunted sourly; but when the marshal reached for the tray he added, "If this is the last one, Henry, when do I get paid? I ain't had a cryin' dime, all these meals I've been fixing."

The marshal made a sour face. "Don't look at me. I told you before, this is a county prisoner."

The cook, scowling, turned to the sheriff. "Well, *somebody's* got to pay the bill! I ain't givin' charity to no damned outlaw!"

"Put in a claim," the lawman said curtly. "But don't bother me now—there's no time." He jerked his head at his deputies. One of them held open the screen so that Marshal Dobbs could edge outside carrying the tray. Then they were gone, moving across the dusty window and disappearing in a diminishing rumble of boots along the boardwalk. The cook, staring after them, swore angrily and made unnecessary racket as he began collecting dirty dishes.

Joe Elliott set down his coffee cup, too excited suddenly to hold it.

If that was the last meal there couldn't be any question. They were moving Bart Dolan to the county seat—and they were doing it now, this afternoon! Once in the jail at Newton, there was no way anyone could help him. So, whatever Joe hoped to do, he was going to have to act quick.

Yet he made himself sit where he was, chewing away at the stale doughnut and forcing coffee down a throat that didn't want to swallow—he didn't dare attract any more attention than he already had, or seem in too big a hurry to leave on the heels of the lawmen.

He waited until the cup was drained, and he had stuffed the last of the doughnut into his mouth. He muttered something to the cook, then, and slid off his stool and made for the door on trembling legs.

Joe Elliott didn't know this country at all. He didn't know the road to Newton, and there was damned little time now to scout it out—he had to figure the sheriff would be starting north with his prisoner, immediately Bart had been able to finish off a skimpy meal.

He picked his spot as best he could, finally settling on a place where the wagon road dipped to ford a sluggish, drought-shrunken stream. The near bank lacked cover, so he took the crossing and dismounted where there were cotton-wood and alder and a few feathery-leafed locusts. Tying his horse out of sight, he climbed the bank and took up a post for himself that commanded a view of the brown land to the south and the sweep of the wagon ruts cutting across it. He sank down against a cottonwood while he took out Vince Choate's gun and checked its loads.

Just three bullets left! Damn it, if he'd had the sense of a jaybird he'd have grabbed the shell belt and holster, too, off that roof-post nail in Belle Starr's barn; but somehow the thought hadn't occurred to him. Afterward, he simply hadn't had the money to stop somewhere along the line and buy himself extra ammunition.

So it meant he'd be going into this with a half-empty gun. . . .

It was breathless under the trees; the heat seemed to collect here, in a buzzing of a million insects and with the dark, sour scent of decay rising from the drying creekbank mud. Time dragged interminably and the sweat broke and ran down his body. All kinds of speculations began running riot through his head: Maybe he'd misinterpreted what he saw and heard, back there in Flint Rock. Or, maybe he'd been spotted and his intentions guessed, so that the sheriff had made a change in his plans—perhaps even chosen some other route. It was a dismal thought, of his one opportunity wasted, and it came near to throwing him into despair.

Then, far off along the stretch of wagon ruts, his anxious gaze became aware of a faint yellow stain of dust against the pale sky. At once he was on his feet, gun in hand, scarcely breathing in the effort of focusing on that dust plume. After what seemed an interminable time, it was close enough that he could make out a dark blur traveling under it; then this shaped itself into a wagon and team, with a single rider following close in their wake.

Suddenly Joe's heart began to pound. He turned once, to check the position of the buckskin that was peacefully grazing where he had tied it to a willow. He looked back again, and, in that one instant, the approaching rig seemed to have leaped so much closer that now he could see the pair of men on the seat, and the third who rode behind them, facing the tailgate.

In the same look, Joe caught a smear of sunlight off a shotgun barrel, on the knees of the man next the driver; he swallowed, in a throat gone dry.

No mistaking that bulky shape: That was the sheriff. He had one of his deputies handling the leathers, the second riding escort. And then Joe Elliott knew there couldn't be any doubt about the prisoner in the wagonbed—the man he could see there, with his head hanging and his whole body rocking loosely to the hard jolting.

It was Bart!

CHAPTER X

It was Bart Dolan, but so plainly weakened and drained by suffering that his brother's throat clogged. The Bart he knew had always seemed strong, and arrogant; seeing him like this—brought low by a bullet—the alarming thought crossed Joe's mind that maybe there was no hope, now, of accomplishing what he'd hoped to.

Still, he couldn't turn back without making a try. Fumbling with the cloth he'd tied about his neck, he pulled it up across his mouth and sweating cheeks, covering the whole lower part of his face. He tugged at his hatbrim, switched the gun to his free hand a moment while he wiped the palm dry against a pantleg. Then he took the weapon again in a firm grip.

The wagon was so close now that he could see the sheriff's pockmarked jaw bulge, working on a chew of tobacco; the deputy's "Whoa!" sounded clearly as he pulled in the horses to a stand at the far edge of the creek. The horses dipped their muzzles toward the muddy water, and the men stirred and eased their positions on the seat. Only the prisoner remained without moving or lifting his hanging head.

The second deputy had moved up alongside the halted rig, now, to let his mount have rein-length so it could drink. Joe could hear the men talking in casual tones, while the horses rested. All this was what he had expected and counted on. Quietly he eased out of the shadow of the cottonwood, six-shooter leveled. He lifted his voice to send it through the mask and past the constriction in his throat.

"All right! Don't nobody make a move!"

For a moment, no one did. He saw them stiffen; next, all but Bart were slowly turning their heads to search for him at the edge of the trees, beyond the shimmering of sunlight on water. Joe swallowed. He called anxiously, "Bart! Can you hear me?"

And the prisoner's head lifted. There was just the glimpse of his face—a blur of white, beneath a shading hatbrim—before the sheriff suddenly went into motion, grabbing up the shotgun that lay across his knees. Tension leaped along Joe Elliott's taut nerves, and cramped his finger on the trigger. Powder smoke whipped into his eyes. But it had been a wild shot, without a target; and then he heard the *b-room* of the shotgun.

The range was too great for such a weapon and the sheriff must have known it; against a steadier hand he might have been dead in the next instant. The lawman was obviously a fighter, though, and this was Joe Elliott's baptism of fire. As buckshot peppered the cottonwood trunk and rattled in the branches overhead, a scared reflex sent him ducking for cover.

It was a signal for the pair of deputies to spring into action. Joe could see the whole thing going to pieces if he didn't act instantly. He caught a glimpse, like a still picture, of sun-smeared water, of the sheriff on his feet in the wagon with the shotgun at shoulder, of the mounted man starting to bring up a hand gun from his belt. Then he steadied, somehow, and pulled off a second hasty shot.

And, stung by the bullet, one of the wagon horses went crazy.

Its scream of pain and terror chilled Joe Elliott's blood. All at once the driver had his hands more than full, with both animals rearing and tangling in the harness. The sheriff gave a yell and reached for a grabiron as the rig threatened to overturn; missing it, he was spun off his feet and dumped sprawling across the seat of the wagon, yet managed in some way to keep his grip on the shotgun. Joe, seeing that, was starting to level his six-shooter again when a flash of sunlight on handcuff steel checked him.

The wounded prisoner had found the strength somewhere to haul himself to his knees. Joe caught his breath as he saw his brother straighten and fling himself full upon the sheriff, and after that the two men were struggling, grappling for possession of that shotgun. The driver, on the seat next to them, was too busy with his team to make any attempt to interfere—but there was still the fellow on the horse, already crowding in now and trying to get close enough to lend his chief a hand.

Joe didn't give him the chance. Shaking loose of a momentary paralysis, he flipped his smoking gun over and felt the kick of it against his wrist. The mounted man lurched violently; he lost his own weapon and it fell with a splash into the creek, as he grabbed at the saddle horn to keep from following it. Almost on the instant, a sleeve of his shirt began to turn bright red.

In that same moment, Bart Dolan had suddenly let go his hold on the shotgun. He lashed out with both fists and the steel manacles, stretched tight, struck the sheriff squarely in the face with an ugly, meaty sound that reached even to where Joe Elliott stood. The lawman fell loosely backward; the shotgun slipped from his grasp, but Bart Dolan managed to catch it before it could slide off the wagon seat.

Too late, the driver had his team yelled into some kind of order and was just starting to turn on the seat, grabbing for a holster. He froze as the shotgun's twin muzzles rammed hard into his back.

"That's being sensible!" Bart told him. "Take your gun out, now, and drop it into the crick. Slow and careful!"

He was as careful about it as anyone could have asked; even at that distance, Joe could see the scared look on his face and the trembling of his hands. When the gun had splashed into the water, Bart Dolan reached and got the sheriff's Colt. He was panting hard from the fighting, but now with his enemies disarmed he could let down a trifle. As his breathing settled he lifted a glance toward Joe Elliott. "Thanks, friend," he called hoarsely. "Whoever you are!"

Joe didn't try to answer. He was feeling the aftermath; there was a trembling in all his limbs, and his face streamed with sweat behind its mask.

The sheriff was beginning to recover now from the blow he'd taken with those handcuffs. He stirred groggily, showing a face smeared with blood, and turning looked directly into the muzzle of his own six-shooter. "Don't try anything!" Bart warned him. "I won't fool with you. Just pass it over."

"What?"

"The key to these bracelets, damn you!"

"I haven't got it."

Bart's stare turned dangerous. "Mister, I won't ask you again!"

"It's the truth," the lawman insisted. "The key's at Newton —in a drawer of my desk. I always figure something like this can happen. I play it safe." He spread his hands. "You think I'm lying, you can search me."

Bart seemed stricken, unwilling to believe it. "Damn' right I'll search you! Turn out your pockets!" He raised his eyes to spear the sheriff's men. "All three of you . . ."

Only when they had complied, without producing anything that looked like a key, did he appear to accept the state of things. He cursed, his voice trembling in fury for a moment; such was his disappointment that Joe thought he meant to club the sheriff with the barrel of his own six-gun. But then, shrugging, he said heavily, "Looks like I'm stuck with these things a while!"

He turned to glance at Joe, who still kept his post on the bank across the creek. "Friend," he said, "I'll thank you to keep this bunch covered. Don't give them any chances."

"Sure thing," Joe agreed. Only after he said it did he remember, in sudden shock, that the gun he held was empty— had been shot dry. By then it was too late to say anything, for Bart had already turned the prisoners over to him. He caught his breath and held it, sweating and fearful that they might somehow guess the truth.

Fortunately, no one seemed inclined to make trouble. They sat quiet enough as Bart broke down the shotgun and flung the separate pieces into the creek. Afterward he picked up the six-shooter he'd laid aside, and climbed out of the wagon over the big wheel, moving with an effort and a painful slowness that told the state of his half-healed wound. Working awkwardly with manacled hands, he proceeded to unfasten the tugs hitching the team to the wagon.

"You got a horse, I suppose?" he called over to Joe.

"He's tied back here."

"Get him."

Joe hurried through the trees to where the buckskin waited. When he came splashing across the shallow ford, he discovered that Bart had forced the second deputy to dismount and was already in the saddle and waiting, the borrowed gun covering his prisoners.

"Maybe you win this time, Dolan," the sheriff was saying, glaring darkly at him from his place on the wagon seat. "But it don't mean anything. Your string's about played out. You and Beecher won't last another six months."

Stubble-bearded, his boldly handsome face showing, in its pallor, the suffering he had undergone since his wounding and capture, Bart still had spirit enough to hold himself tall in the stirrups, and scoff at the lawman's prediction. "There was a Pinkerton man come to take a look at me in that jail," he said. "He tried to tell me the same thing."

"You better believe it! Wild animals like you and Beecher are out of date. The country can't put up with you any longer. Even Jesse James finally got it—and we'll get *you*, if we have to take an army down into the Nations and dig you out!"

"Come right ahead," Bart Dolan said with harsh confidence, and turned as Joe Elliott rode up beside him.

Joe still wore his handkerchief mask, but at these close quarters he didn't have much confidence in it—not under the weight of the sheriff's keen stare. "I'm ready if you are," he said.

"Bring the horses."

Joe nodded; he got the wagon team by their harness, as Bart told the lawmen, "A little walk won't hurt you any—or, you could just sit in the wagon until somebody comes along." There was no answer. In a grim silence Bart Dolan kicked the horse under him—a stockinged black with good lines, that looked made for endurance—and circled the stalled rig. Joe fell in behind, leading the captured wagon horses, and they rode away from there.

They rode south, across a field, the motionless wagon slowly dwindling behind them to a dark speck against the green of the creek timber. Then their passage dropped into a swale, and stream and wagon and lawmen were lost from sight.

In all that time, neither man had spoken. Joe sensed that Bart had been concentrating on holding himself in the saddle, trying not to show what it was costing him. Now, however, he pulled rein and his shoulders sagged as though giving way to a weight that rested on them.

The younger man said anxiously, "That bullet bothering you?"

Bart nodded. He lifted a hand to touch his chest, high up on the left, and winced. "It's pure hell," he muttered, "the way a little thing like that can—"

And then his words broke off, as Joe Elliott pulled the mask down from across his face.

"*You!*"

The other nodded, and wiped a hand across the dust and sweat that smeared his cheeks. "Yeah. It's me, Bart."

"But, kid! Why, how in the name of God—!"

It was too big a subject to go into now. Joe turned for a look behind as he said nervously, "Can't that wait? There's things we should be doing!"

"You ain't worried about any two-bit sheriff?" Bart retorted, in a tone of scorn. But then he admitted gruffly, "Would have been all up with me, I guess, if you hadn't shown just when you did—however the hell you did it! My luck's not completely used up yet, after all . . ."

His eye lit on the horse Joe straddled. "Hey! Where'd you get that animal? Looks to me like Vince Choate's buckskin!"

His brother nodded. "It is—I borrowed him. Choate and Reb were the only ones got back alive from that train job." He watched his brother's look alter, to this grim news.

It was really alarming, he thought, the change he could see in him in two short years. There had been a fire in Bart Dolan, a devil-may-care dash and reckless gaiety. Now, it was gone. Joe saw instead the face of a man drawn fine by hardship and by the bitter pain of his wound. The bright fire had turned to something else—a fury, a feverish and angry light that might not be entirely sane. It sobered and saddened Joe, to compare this man with the one who had been his idol only a few brief months ago.

Bart took a long breath. "Like you say, we can talk later. Let's hit the road."

Joe said dubiously, "It's a long piece before we reach the Nations. Over fifty miles. You sure you can make it?"

"I'll make it," his brother said grimly. "We'll hole up by day and do our traveling by night."

"Hole up!" The other blinked. "Where, for God's sake? In country as settled as this?"

Bart shot him a look that stopped his tongue; it was a hot and angry glare, accepting no argument. "I know what I'm doing!" he snapped. "So just shut up and let me handle this."

Joe blinked once, swallowed. "All right. Sure, Bart."

"But I got to get rid of these damned things!" He held up his wrists, linked by the steel handcuffs. His fists clenched and Joe saw them tremble; abruptly he lowered them again, picked up the reins. "Well, come along. You can bring them horses of the sheriff's—we'll ditch them after an hour or so, make better time."

His mouth closed firmly as he pulled the black around. And Joe knew already he was going to do exactly as he was told.

CHAPTER XI

That was the beginning of a nightmare.

It had been a great part of the legend of men like Bart Dolan—men like Reb Beecher, and Jesse James—that they were able to hit a bank or a railroad and then make a bewildering and ground-eating run for it, burning up distance like a scorching wind and losing pursuit before it had a fair chance to get organized. Once, maybe, it had really been like that—once when this country had been as open and empty of settlement as it still was a little farther west, out Union City way. But not around here any longer, not now. Here, in this southeastern corner of Kansas, the years had seen great changes. Homesteaders' plows and barbed wire had been at work, cutting up the land in neat parcels of a quarter section or even less. Here there would be no more hell-for-leather flights across open country, the wind blowing strong against a man's face and a posse losing itself in his dust. Instead, Joe and Bart found themselves caught up in a kind of grotesque parody of the legends—a checkerboard maze of wire and straight-ruled section-line roads that held them to a painful crawl.

They might lift an occasional gate, to cut through some farmer's back pasture in a long detour and avoid one of the many drab little farm villages; but mostly they had to stick to the roads, where ever so often they would pass a rider or an overalled farmer driving a creaking wagon. Each time this happened, the sweat would run cold over Joe Elliott's ribs as he waited for a sign of recognition, or at the very least to have a curious eye notice the sick pallor in Bart Dolan's face, the telltale shine of the manacles on his wrists. But they got no more than passing looks and careless nods of greeting.

Plainly, the news of Bart Dolan's escape hadn't had time to spread, yet. No one saw anything suspicious in a pair of dusty horsemen, lagging southward through the tail end of the sweltering August day.

Bart Dolan kept doggedly on, and it was only the gray cast to his face and the drag of his shoulders that warned Joe how much grim effort he was putting into this ride. He had no energy to spare for talk, and after a few tentative attempts Joe gave it up. He merely kept an anxious regard on his brother, ready to move in close and lend a hand if exhaustion threatened to overcome him. Yet the hours dragged out and still Bart maintained the steady, slogging pace. He had reserves of pure brute courage, apparently, that kept him going.

The sun flirted with the long horizon, then slid behind it in a smear of fiery color; and it was like the door of a blast furnace being swung shut, over there. But the heat remained, nearly undiminished. Twilight was spreading when, at a crossroads, Bart Dolan finally pulled rein and Joe saw him studying the land in frowning concentration.

This was new country to Joe Elliott, a different route from the one he'd taken when he made his lonely probe north to Flint Rock in search of his brother. He'd assumed Bart knew where he was going. Now he felt the belly-tightening of doubt and apprehension at the thought that they might be lost, in hostile territory.

But he kept his silence, letting Bart work out the problem. And now there was the musical tinkling of a cowbell, and an old man came plodding barefooted toward them leading a brindle-hided animal on a neckrope. Watery eyes blinked sharply at these two strange horsemen, but he would have gone by without pausing except that Bart Dolan suddenly asked, "Pop, which way is Winfield?"

The old fellow halted to look at them again. He jerked a thumb over his shoulder. "Down thataway—but it's a good piece."

The cow swung its head; the soft tone of the bell dropped into evening quiet. Bart indicated the crossing and said, "Where's this other road go?"

"Toward Andover. And Augusty." Curiosity deepened in the red-rimmed eyes. "You two lost, or something?"

"Just a little mixed up, for a minute. Thanks." Joe Elliott's heart lost track of a beat, as he saw his brother start to raise a hand in casual salute; but Bart must have remembered in time and quickly dropped it again, and Joe didn't think the old-timer could have seen the metal bracelets. Bart flicked him a glance and a summoning jerk of the head, and turned his horse into the Andover road and kicked it with spurless heels. Following, Joe was painfully aware of the ancient still staring after them, still holding his cow by the neckrope, until a slight dip in the road dropped him out of sight.

"That old fellow's going to remember us!" he said darkly as he caught up.

Bart pulled up a moment, to glance back toward the sunset-streaked horizon. They sat their horses with the dusk thickening slowly around them. "Maybe you want we should go back and take care of him?"

Joe Elliott blinked. "No!" he exclaimed hastily. "Hell, no!

I didn't mean *that!* It's just that we better hurry, wherever it is you're taking us!" He peered ahead, where shadows were already settling across the dusty earth. "Did you learn what you wanted to know?"

Getting no answer, he shot a look at his brother's face, and saw that it was as gray as the dusk, seemingly scraped clean of every spare scrap of flesh. He said in alarm, "Bart! You all right? You don't look good at all!"

The steel bracelets clinked softly as Bart lifted both hands to his face and rubbed a palm across beard stubble. He took a long breath, and his tired body straightened in the saddle. He said bluntly, "Don't worry about me, kid. They ain't done for me, yet. I ain't figuring to kick out what's left of my life in some backcountry road in Kansas—I promise you that!"

But as they started on Joe held back a little, lagging a pace or two behind the other horse. Through the gloom he watched that other figure, waiting for the first warning sag that would get him to Bart in time to prevent him tumbling from the saddle. . . .

Hours passed. Night settled fully on the prairie; yellow lamplight winked at them from farmhouse windows and then, later yet, the lamps went out, one by one and they were left with starlight, and a moon coming on to the full. But still they kept moving, painfully slow, men and horses alike at the near edge of exhaustion.

Joe lost all track of time. He thought it must have been midnight or later when Bart reined in before a dark and silent farmstead that looked like a dozen others they had seen—the house set back at the end of a dimly marked access lane, a barn and a few sheds grouped about it. As they studied the place their horses drooped under them, too tired by now even to pull at the rank, dead grass that grew between the road ruts.

Saddle leather creaked to Bart's shift of position. "See anything moving?"

Puzzled, Joe waited. "Looks safe enough," Bart mumbled finally, and kneed his horse over to the gate. Leaning from saddle he fumbled at it, slipped free the loop of wire that held it closed. With a faint, creaking protest the gate sagged open.

"Hey! What are you doing?" Joe Elliott demanded.

He got no answer. Bart simply walked his horse through the opening and, without looking back, started down the dim lane toward the farm; and there was no choice except to assume he knew what he was up to.

Smothering a curse, Joe moved to follow, then remembered and had to turn back and swing the gate shut, holding it with his knee while he forced the loop of wire in place to fasten it. By the time this was done he had been left behind. Anxious to catch up, he kicked his buckskin into a jog—and just then heard a dog start up a ferocious barking, yonder at the buildings. The sound started the sweat on him and sent his hand to the butt of the gun at his belt.

The barking grew louder as he neared. In a window of the house, yellow lamplight sprang to life and, a moment later, a door opened. A woman's voice spoke: "Shep! What's wrong, Shep? Be quiet, boy!"

Joe could see the dog now, a small dark shadow whipping back and forth through the dense shadows as it worried Bart's horse and made the night hideous with its hysterical yelping. He saw the woman, too. She stood in the doorway, a wrapper or some other light-colored garment pulled tight around her. She scolded the dog again, then fell silent as the black, bearing Bart Dolan, lagged to a halt at the edge of the lamplight. Suddenly she was turning to call someone in the house behind her: "Bring the lamp. Hurry!"

The dog was still making a noise and trying to take nips at the black's heels. The horse sidestepped uneasily and Bart said, "Whoa, now!" Joe saw another person edge into the door beside the woman—this one a boy, barely as high as her elbow, and carrying an oil lamp. Its glow picked out the tall figure of Bart Dolan as the latter took right foot from stirrup, swung it up and across the cantle of his saddle.

The instant his boot touched earth the dog darted in, only to fall abruptly silent and begin to wag its tail. Before Joe had more than a moment to notice this, he saw his brother sway and break at the knees, staggering against his horse. The woman cried out. And, moving fast though his own body was stiff from the hours of riding, Joe tumbled out of saddle in time to keep him from sagging limply to the ground.

The woman came hurrying, carrying the lamp that she'd taken from the boy's hands. The upward glow of it shone streakily on Bart's face, showing the dust and the sweat and the dark beard stubble—and the slack features, the glazed eyes.

Bart Dolan was a big man. For a moment, as the black horse shifted its hoofs and moved away, the sudden weight of him almost broke Joe's grip. He managed to get a better hold, and heard the woman's quick gasp: "Oh! Be careful! Is—is he badly hurt?"

"Hard to say."

Joe himself was still held in the grip of puzzlement. "Do you know this man? You know who he is?"

"Of course." They stood close together, with Bart supported between them, and Joe could feel the woman's eyes on his face. "But, I'd heard the law had him. And if you were a lawman—you'd never have brought him here!"

"I'm no lawman," he answered. Dimly, he thought it was beginning to make sense. Bart had kept talking about holing up somewhere. Strange as it seemed, this farmhouse must have been the goal he was making for, all that time.

The woman said, "We must get him inside. Tommy, you take the horses."

"Hold on!" Joe snatched the reins away from the boy's hand. "Where's he think he'll be taking them?"

"Why, only to the barn."

85

He was still dubious, still suspicious. "Just don't be in too big of a hurry! I got to know first, who else is here?"

"No one but myself and the children." The woman placed a reassuring hand on his arm. "Believe me—it's all right. If you're his friend, then you're in no danger."

There was nothing to do but trust her. He was practically dead on his feet himself, and Bart presented a problem that was just too much for him to manage. "Hold the lamp, then," he said gruffly. "So I can see what I'm doing . . ."

He ducked his head and got Bart's limp arm around his shoulders. Staggering a little under his brother's weight, he directed Bart's half-conscious steps toward the house.

The woman moved ahead of them, carrying the light; shadows fled before it and showed him a meager kitchen, much like Abel Quitman's. A door stood open on a tiny bedroom; through it he caught a glimpse of a brass bedstead and rumpled bedclothing, and a tousle-headed little girl sitting up rubbing her eyes and blinking at the lamp. Joe got his brother as far as the oilcloth-covered kitchen table and one of the tall, ladderbacked chairs. Bart dropped into it and propped himself there, his head lying limp against the back of it; in the light of the lamp the woman set on the table, his strong face looked emaciated—the eyes sunken, the prominent cheekbones and jaw seeming ready to burst through the stretched white skin.

"It's the bullet hole in his chest," Joe said dully. "Sheriff tried to move him to the county seat before he was in shape to travel. I got him away, but he's been in the saddle for ten hours or more."

She was already at work undoing the front of the hurt man's shirt. She laid it open, revealing a bandage—once clean enough, but now darkened by grime and sweat. From a sewing basket on the table she took a pair of scissors and with quick efficiency snipped the cloth away. Joe Elliott held his breath.

He let it out again, in a long sigh. The wound was an ugly one, all right, puckered and purple with healing tissue; but it seemed to be holding. At least there was no seepage of blood, no indication that it was in danger of tearing open. The woman laid a strong brown hand against the hurt man's chest and Bart stirred, his head moving against the back of the chair. She took her hand away again, nodding. "It could be a lot worse."

It was as though a burden had been lifted from both of them. Joe found his legs were suddenly trembling so that he had to take hold of a chairback to steady him. At once the woman's touch was resting gently on his shoulder and she said, "You're as tired as he is. Probably starved, too."

"I could eat."

She didn't have to pressure him to sit. He dropped into the chair and watched, from eyes dulled with fatigue, as she moved first to pull a curtain over the window, and then set about building a fire in the range.

It could have been any typical Kansas homesteader's kitchen, except for the neatness and cleanliness. This woman seemed to have Mary Quitman's knack for making do with little—it was a talent Mary had been forced to develop because of her uncle's stinginess, but in this case Joe suspected that what he saw was the pinch of real poverty. The oilcloth on the table was scrubbed white and threadbare. The window curtain looked as though it had been patched, though carefully and neatly; so did the wrapper the woman wore belted closely about her. Her feet were bare on the scrubbed pine floorboards.

She must be in her early thirties, judging from the size of her children. The little girl had come into the bedroom doorway, now, and stood knuckling the sleep from her eyes as she stared solemnly at the man at the table—a small, black-haired miniature of her mother, with brown eyes that looked big enough to drown in. A hard existence must have aged the woman, Joe thought, fining her down and roughening her hands, and fading the luster from hair that was as dark as her daughter's.

With the fire going, she pulled a coffeepot onto the front of the stove. Soon a pan of leftover stew was heating and the mingled aromas began working at Joe's salivary glands. Having dipped water from a barrel and set it on to heat, the woman got out a tea towel and began tearing it into strips for a clean bandage. She looked at Joe thoughtfully as her hands worked.

She said, "You really took him away from the law? All alone?"

He felt himself coloring slightly. "There was only the sheriff and a couple of deputies. I got the drop while they was watering their horses, and gave Bart a chance to grab the sheriff's shotgun. It wasn't much of a trick after that."

"All I know is, you must be a very good friend. I never thought anyone in that bunch he runs with would risk so much!"

He hesitated. "I'm his brother," he said, and saw her fine eyes widen.

"Not Joe Elliott! Why didn't I guess?" She answered his unspoken question: "Bart's told us so much about you."

"Have you known him long?" Joe asked, really curious.

"Just a little over a year now, I guess. He came riding by one day, on a horse that badly needed a shoe. My husband was a blacksmith, before we homesteaded, and I have his tools out in the barn . . ."

She broke off as the boy, Tommy, came running in with the black-and-white mutt at his heels, to report that the horses were unsaddled and watered and fed. His mother sent him scampering out again after an armload of firewood, and then told Joe Elliott, "Lenson's our name. I'm Rose Lenson. That little monkey in the doorway," she added, catching sight of her, "is Alice. Back to bed with you, now!" She scooped the child into her arms. "Everything's all right."

Still too fogged with sleep to protest, the little girl let herself be carried into the bedroom. Her mother returned, closing the door behind her.

Joe asked her, "The kids' father? He ain't around?"

"Sam Lenson died of pneumonia, three winters ago." It was not a plea for sympathy, merely a statement of fact, but it went far to explaining what he had seen of the poverty she must struggle with, the burdens that put the tiredness in her eyes and in the line of her shoulders.

At the table, Bart Dolan suddenly stirred and lifted his head, peered around him with unseeing and startled eyes. "Rose!" he called harshly.

Quickly she came to him, touched his shoulder and said, in a way that seemed the same to Joe as when she had spoken to soothe the child: "I'm here. It's all right. You're perfectly safe. You just sit still while I see about that bandage; then there'll be something to eat."

Bart tried to lift a hand and the steel bracelets clinked. He looked down at his wrists; his mouth twisted, angry and hard. "These damned things—!"

"You said something about blacksmith tools," Joe remarked. "I reckon getting them off is more important to him just now than food, or anything else."

Rose Lenson said, "Let me finish here first. It won't take but a minute . . ."

She was already at work. With warm water from the stove, she carefully bathed the puckered bullet wound in Bart's chest. He sat quietly and let her work, only wincing a couple of times as she bound it tight in clean strips of cloth ripped from the towel. The boy, Tommy, had returned now with an armload of kindling, which he tossed clattering into the box by the stove and then stood by, watching, his dark eyes large with interest and concern. Finally, able to contain himself no longer, he blurted, "Is Uncle Bart gonna be all right, Maw?"

"Of course," Rose Lenson told her son, smiling at him briefly. She made a final knot and pulled the shirt into place across the bandage. Bart began to fumble with the buttons and Tommy's glance dropped to the big man's hands.

"Hey! What's that you got on your wrists?"

The hands went still. But Rose Lenson, stepping in, gave her son's shoulder a push that turned him away, toward the loft ladder in a corner of the room. "Little boys shouldn't ask so many questions," she scolded him, not unkindly. "Now, you get back to bed, you hear me? A body'd think there wasn't going to be any work that needed doing here, come morning!"

"Sure, Maw." Still curious but obedient, the youngster gathered his dog under one arm and went scrambling up the ladder. Joe Elliott, looking at Bart, asked, "He hasn't been told who you really are?"

"Of course not!" the other man said gruffly. "Far as the kids are concerned I'm their Uncle Bart, that drops in once in a while. Think I can have them blabbing it to the neighbors that Bart Dolan has been to their house?" But Joe had an intuition there was more to it than that. He'd been watching the other's face as the boy was asking his anxious questions; he'd seen the sudden guilt and discomfort when Bart knew Tommy had caught a glimpse of those handcuffs. He had a hunch his brother thought a lot of Rose Lenson's children, and that he was shamed and humiliated to think of them seeing him in irons. . . .

Bart lumbered to his feet now, leaning heavily on the table as he did so. "Come on, kid," he muttered. "Let's get out there to the barn and knock these damned things off.

"I tell you, I can't stand 'em another minute. They're gonna drive me crazy!"

CHAPTER XII

The handcuffs gave a lot of trouble. They resisted Joe's best efforts with cold chisel and maul, as he and Bart knelt in the straw with the anvil between them; but after a lock finally gave to the battering, Bart was able to free one hand and hold the chisel himself, directing the blows for greater effect. At last the twisted metal fell away and he flung it aside and settled back onto his heels, chafing raw and bleeding wrists.

"That's better!" he grunted. "That's one hell of a lot better!"

Joe got to his feet and laid the maul on the bench where he had found it. A lantern, on the floor beside them, cast their shadows against the deeper darkness of the barn interior. They could hear their horses nuzzling the feed Tommy had put down for them. Outside, the hot summer night was completely silent.

Sleeving sweat from his forehead, Joe said, "I'm sorry I couldn't do a neater job. Afraid I bunged you up some."

"It's all right, kid." Bart squinted up at him. Somehow, in the lantern glow, his face seemed more like what Joe remembered—the strong features, the firm yet humorous shape of the mouth, the creases at the corners of deep-set eyes. "Come to think of it," he said suddenly, "I guess no one has to tell you what it feels like, wearing a pair of them things."

Joe looked down at his own wrists, in memory feeling the shackles there as plainly as though it had been yesterday that he wore them. "It humiliates a man," he said slowly. "It cuts him down, makes an animal out of him. That's the worst of it."

"Yeah." Bart flexed his arms. He had a limp, near-empty bag of tobacco in his shirt pocket, that someone must have given him while he sat in the Flint Rock jail. He pulled it out and made himself a smoke, then offered the tobacco to Joe who shook his head. Bart put the sack away, jacked up the lantern and lit his cigarette. He dragged deep at it.

"Now!" he said, the cigarette bobbing on his lips. "I get some food inside me, and a few hours sleep—I might begin to feel almost human!"

"And after that?"

Bart squinted at him, through the upward drift of smoke. "Right now I'm too bushed even to care!"

Joe was almost ready to agree.

Waking, he could have believed he was back in his cubby-hole in Quitman's barn. Bars of morning sunlight, swimming with dustmotes, slanted down at him where he lay in a sweet-smelling bed he'd burrowed out for himself in the hay. In their stalls, the chestnut and the black were stirring, munching grain. Joe sat up, rubbing his face, and looked over at the other man still curled in sleep.

They could have shared the loft with the boy, Tommy, but it had seemed wiser to stay near their horses. Besides, Joe felt there was another idea in his brother's mind: If by some unlucky chance they should be trailed here and discovered, it was a protection for the Lensons if the two of them could appear to have sneaked into the barn without any knowledge or connivance of the widow and her children.

Good reasoning, Joe thought.

He placed another sound that had roused him—someone was graining the chickens. He got up, stretching cramped muscles, and walked over to the barn door. One leaf stood open giving him a view of the yard, and of the house with a wispy feather of smoke trailing from its mud chimney. The sky was high and white, the day starting with the full weight of the August sun.

Now he had the first good look at the Lenson place and saw for the first time, clearly, just how poverty-stricken it really was. The house had been painted once, but so long ago that Kansas weather had scoured it down to the bare boards. The roof lacked shingles, the fences needed mending; almost everywhere he looked, he saw the absence and the need of a man's touch. All told, it was mute testimony to what Rose Lenson was up against, trying to maintain this homestead since her husband's death.

Then he saw her, in a long homespun skirt and apron, sleeves rolled above her elbows. She had a pan of grain in the bend of one arm, her other hand raised to shade her eyes. "Good morning!" she called cheerily. He answered and walked over to her, and a score of busy chickens clucked and fluttered out of his way. The two of them stood in the sun, with the birds around their feet pecking at the yellow grain the woman scattered to them from time to time.

"I hope you rested," she said.

"Never better. I was tireder than I knew. Bart, too, I guess—at least he's still sleeping."

Her eyes clouded. "Poor man! Isn't it enough to break your heart? To see someone as strong, and as big as that—laid so low!"

"Some people would say he got no more than he deserved.

Maybe, even, that it's too bad the bullet didn't go a little straighter."

"He's a human being," she answered stoutly. "But I suppose I know a side of him most people have never had a chance to know!"

"Yeah." Suddenly he couldn't say anything more. His tongue clove to the roof of his mouth, and as her brown eyes looked into his he felt the heat begin to beat up through his cheeks. He would have looked away but couldn't, something in her level regard holding him—ashamed to turn from it.

"I know what you're thinking," Rose Lenson told him quietly.

"I never said—!"

"You don't need to. Oh, I'm not angry," she went on, her voice unhurried, her grave expression unchanged. "I know what anyone is bound to think who sees a lonely widow befriending a man and taking him into her home." She held up her hand and he saw the glint of gold. "But I've never yet dishonored this ring, or the memory of the man who placed it on my finger. Not with your brother, or with anyone else. That's the truth."

"Be none of my damn' business," he blurted gruffly, "even if it wasn't. But I'm sure it is."

She smiled her thanks. "I won't deny thinking, sometimes, how things might have been different. I know Bart feels the same way about it. He's even spoken of marriage . . ."

"To an outlaw? You couldn't do that!"

"Probably not. Oh, I don't know!" Rose shook her head, tossed out the last of the grain and let the pan fall empty to her side. She looked around the bare and dreary yard of her home.

Joe read her thoughts. "I guess, at times, almost anything might look better than this . . . Don't you have any help, at all?"

"But of course," she said with forced brightness. "During

the harvest I can sometimes hire a hand to do the heavy work. And Tommy's big enough, now, he can almost handle a man's share. He's really a lot of help. We get along fine."

He thought of the half-grown youngster, and saw the many things here that needed a man's attention, and his heart went out completely to Rose Lenson and her uncomplaining brand of courage.

She touched his hand, and gathered her full skirts. "Come to the house whenever you're ready for breakfast. I'll put something together."

"Thanks." He hesitated. "You wouldn't have such a thing as a razor around the place?"

"Of course. My husband's. I'll get it out."

Joe stood and watched her move away from him across the sun-baked yard, a trim, square-shouldered figure of a woman, with the first touches of gray showing in the black pile of her hair. A pretty fine person, he thought. He waved to the little girl who met her mother in the doorway, and after the door had swung shut on them he turned and waded through clucking chickens and entered the barn. He hauled up short, staring at the gun Bart Dolan sat holding on him.

When he saw who it was, Bart made a grimace and lowered the weapon, with a grunt. He brushed away a wisp of straw that clung to one cheek. "Sorry," he grunted. "I was only half-awake. Shows how jumpy I am!"

He laid the gun aside and began pulling on his boots. Joe came and placed his shoulder against the roof prop and leaned there. "How do you feel?" he asked, and got a mere nod in answer. "Everything seems to be under control," he reported. "The horses are rested and look ready for travel again. I figure if the law was going to find us here, it would have done it by now."

Bart seemed to consider this in silence as he grunted over drawing on the boots. He got up and stomped around in them a moment to settle them, picked up his hat. "I stick to my original plan," he said. "Stay here till dark, then pull out. What you do is up to you." He put the weight of those deep-set eyes upon his brother.

The other hesitated. "I been figuring I'd string with you a while, Bart. If you'll let me."

"*Let* you! After what you did, yesterday? That's a hell of a way to put it!" The bleak, harsh lines of Bart's face gentled a trifle, so that Joe could see behind the mask some trace of the devil-may-care, generous nature that he had remembered from two years before. "I ain't ever going to forget, kid!" he said softly. "Not another man in the world would have risked his neck for me—least of all, any of that scum of Reb Beecher's! If I ain't rightly said, 'Thank you,' it's because the right words to say it just ain't in my vocabulary!"

Confused and pleased, Joe could only look at the toes of his shoes. If he had ever wondered why he took on that chore, yesterday, the answer was clear enough to him now. For reward, he would never ask anything more than this moment when they were suddenly close together—closer than he had ever really hoped.

He shrugged and said, a little lamely, "I was only glad I could bring it off."

"Naturally, you're welcome to trail with me, if it's what you want," Bart said. "But you better think twice. Take it from me, kid, this ain't much of a life. You've seen enough that you should know that for yourself." Half-consciously, as he spoke, Bart put up a hand to touch the bandage under his shirt. "And if you're worrying about that sheriff—I wouldn't. Way you kept your face covered, I doubt any of those three would ever know you again."

"That's not what bothers me. Maybe you've forgotten, I told you last night—I'm already wanted, for assault and robbery and jumping parole!"

Bart frowned. "Any idea who it was actually done the job?"

"I got better than an idea! It was that fellow Lamb—the stock buyer. He was mad enough at Rick Slaughter, I think he could have killed him. I figure he laid for him and took back the money he lost, and then left town fast. I dunno how I'd ever find him, now—let alone prove anything on him."

"Rough," the older man agreed, shaking his head. "Damned rough. I guess you're right, after all, kid—you got no particular choice, except the Nations. Maybe, later, we can do something about your problem."

"Sure. Maybe," Joe said shortly. He knew it was just a word. No one could do anything.

The long day dragged itself out somehow. Joe and Bart ate the food Rose Lenson cooked, used the long-shanked razor she dug up for them. During most of the time, Bart slept—still gaining back the strength that had been sadly depleted. Joe, however, found himself turning restless; going out into the yard, in early afternoon, he saw the flash of a hoe blade in the truck garden north of the house, where Tommy Lenson was busily chopping weeds and breaking up the dry earth. Joe walked over and took the hoe from him, finding real pleasure in the familiar physical labor of a farm. And he and the boy worked that way through the afternoon, yarning together, Tommy toting buckets of well water for the struggling crops.

The boy had his mother's black hair and grave brown eyes. It was touching to see how hard and steadily he toiled, leaning against the weight of the filled bucket, stumbling over the dry clods. The sun bore down from the white-hot sky, the ground shimmered under it. Once Joe looked over toward the house and saw Rose in the back door, pausing a moment to watch them. He lifted a hand and she responded.

It all made him think of Quitman's, with a great onrush of homesickness—the turkeys gobbling on their wagonbox roost, the big windmill blades turning, and Mary Quitman humming to herself as she moved about the dugout kitchen, maybe doing the week's baking and pretending to be unaware of him constantly keeping track of everything she did. . . .

The hoeing finally done, Joe looked around and found other things he could turn his hand to—man-chores that had gone too long neglected. One leaf of the big barn doors sagged badly; he found tools and rehung it. Then, as the sun lay swollen above the western horizon, he hauled timber up from the woodlot and used the ax to knock it into firewood. He was tired enough, when he finished, but it was a good tiredness and even the thought of a night ride ahead didn't bother him.

Supper, the last meal, was a subdued and silent one, eaten by streaky lamplight though the evening outside still pulsed with the glow of dying day. Only the children seemed to feel like talking. Rose Lenson moved silently between table and stove; her lips were heavy and Joe thought her eyes showed the signs of unshed tears, not far below the surface. He could see her effort to smile at something Tommy said. Bart followed her movements with a brooding look, himself saying next to nothing during the course of the meal.

With the youngsters constantly underfoot, he knew that these two people had had no chance for so much as a moment together; it seemed the least he could do to give them one. Hurrying to finish eating, he swallowed the last of his coffee and pushed his chair back. "Young fellow," he said to Tommy, "how about giving me a hand getting the horses up?"

Tommy got his mother's nod and was on his feet immediately. "Me, too!" cried Alice, as Joe had known she would, and he swept her up into the crook of his arm and carried her squealing from the house. He had made quite a hit with these children, and saddling the horses became a game which he prolonged until, leading them from the barn, he walked into a blood-red smear of afterglow and deepening shadow. Through the kitchen window he could see his brother and the woman still seated at the table, their heads together in earnest talk.

"How come you and Uncle Bart always travel by night?" Tommy wanted to know.

"Cooler that way," he answered absently. He looked down at the little girl who had trailed them from the barn, hugging a bedraggled doll in a faded rag of a dress. The doll had only one arm; Joe Elliott, looking for an excuse to give those two in the kitchen a few precious moments more alone, asked, "What happened here—an accident?"

"Yes." Gravely, from a pocket of her pinafore, her chubby hand fished up the missing arm. Her big eyes watched him as he examined it. "Well, now," he said. "Looks like a job for the doctor."

"You won't hurt her?" Anxiously.

"Wouldn't think of it." Taking out his knife, Joe cut a length of whang from one of his saddle strings. Afterward, squatting on his heels with the children gathered close, he performed the operation, stringing the arm on stout leather and managing to effect a crude jointure. When he was finished, in the last grainy light of dusk, the arm moved stiffly but the doll was whole. "There you are," he said, and the little girl solemnly clutched it to her breast, her dark eyes thanking him.

One of the waiting horses stamped and jingled its harness. A bullbat streaked silently across the sky, that had turned the color of steel. "Time to go." Joe slapped his knees and pushed to a stand.

He scraped his soles as he approached the door, and fumbled with the latch; yet despite his warning, the man and woman standing in the middle of the kitchen were only just moving apart as he pushed the door open and said, "Horses are waiting." Bart looked at him as though he didn't hear or understand. Rose's mouth was still heavy, with the shape of their kiss. But she nodded, and to Bart she said in a voice that was little above a whisper: "You'll be careful?"

He only nodded, and touched her shoulder. She dropped her arms woodenly and let him walk away. She was still standing there, without motion and wearing a look that held no hope, as Bart picked his hat from the table and moved past Joe, into the dusk. Joe looked at the woman for a moment, then quietly closed the door.

He let Bart mount first, stiffly but without hesitation. He passed the reins up, and swung into the buckskin's saddle. "So long, kids," he told the boy and girl.

Bart said nothing.

Joe reined about and they rode out of the yard, with the treble farewells of the children drifting thinly behind them long after they had followed the lane to the road and let themselves through the gate. And then they were alone with the sounds of their horses, and the noise of insects in the weeds beside the road.

"It's no fun to say goodbye," Joe Elliott remarked quietly.

"About as much fun as sticking your arm into the fire!"

After a moment Joe said, "Does it matter any, what I think?"

In the dusk, he saw the other's head lift and turn to him. "All right—what do you think?"

"I think you should say goodbye for good—and then get out of her life and let the woman alone. She loves you. And you can't do anything but hurt her!"

There was the sound of a sharp breath being drawn between tight lips. "Thanks for nothing!" Bart said heavily. "I don't suppose it occurred to you that I might be in love with *her*."

"It occurred to me, all right. Even before she told me you'd spoken about marrying. You wouldn't do a thing like that to her, and to those kids?" He caught himself, then, and shook his head. "Sorry. I'm talking out of turn."

"And why shouldn't I marry her?" Bart Dolan demanded. He pulled his horse around, half across the road, and Joe had to draw rein and listen. "What else do you suppose has been on my mind, for the past year? Except to take the three of them off that piece of hardpan, and out of that house that's about to fall down on them? Take them clear the hell away from this country, to someplace where we can live a normal life—the kind of life I never knew anything about, and never wanted until it was too late! I've got it all figured. Just one job, kid—that's all it takes. One last job!"

"After Wichita?" Joe exclaimed. "I don't see how you could tempt fate by trying it again!"

"Don't you?" Bart reached across the space between the saddles and seized his brother's arm hard, and Joe felt the trembling of the hand, heard the intensity in his voice. "For the first time in my life, kid, I got something worth living for—worth dying for, if it comes to that!

"Do you know how much I have to show, after these years with Beecher? I'll tell you: The clothes I stand in! But I know what I want, and I'm going ahead—because there's only one way in the world I know how to get them. And any man that stands in my way will suffer for it. Any man at all!"

Joe's arm was abruptly released; saddle leather creaked as Bart drew back, managing an uneasy bark of laughter. "What the hell are we arguing about? We got no quarrel. Come on—let's be heading south . . ."

CHAPTER XIII

Younger's Bend had a look of being completely deserted; Joe Elliott, listening to the stillness, felt all the pressures of their flight from Kansas and thought warily of a trap. It was here, after all, that he'd once taken frantic cover to elude a pair of deputy marshals from Hangin' Judge Parker's court. But Bart Dolan seemed beyond caution. When Joe tried to pull up at the foot of the trail, by the covered spring, his companion brushed past him, booting the sweat-shiny black and sending it straight up the hill toward the cabin on the bench. And after an instant's hesitation, Joe could do no more than follow.

Bart was already dismounting as his brother halted in front of the cabin. Joe stepped down more slowly, first taking another searching look around him. A crow flapped overhead and vanished above a ridge behind the cabin. The dark, cool scent of the river came up from the shallows below. There was no sign of anyone around the place; no horses were in the pole corral. Bart sang out, "Hello!" Getting no answer, he moved up onto the shallow porch and through the open door; and, with a shrug, Joe followed him.

The cabin's single room showed its usual disorder—beds not made, the floor unswept. A battered coffeepot hung on the crane but the fireplace held black ashes. Joe said, "You suppose they all cleared out for some reason?"

He dared to hope so. He was not particularly eager for his next encounter with Vince Choate, and he couldn't help but feel that it would be a good thing for Bart if his brother never made connections with Reb Beecher again.

Bart, scowling, prowled the cabin. Joe felt he could see a change in him, in the time since they'd left the Lenson farm. He seemed thinner, gaunted, as though consumed by the days of riding and the effects of his wound. But there was something more than this—a new intensity, an inward fire that seemed to have been kindled by his desperate parting with Rose Lenson. It had turned him moody and given barbs to his temper, and rubbed up a feverish gleam in his eyes. He struck Joe Elliott as a man driven to desperate ends, and there was nothing really to say to him.

He stopped now beside the fireplace, laid a palm against the side of the coffeepot. "Still warm," he muttered. "There must be somebody around . . ."

Suddenly Joe was lifting a hand to silence him. Bart had heard, in the same moment, the footsteps on the porch; he jerked about, one hand moving toward the holstered gun at his waist. Even as they turned to face the door, a shadow crossed it and Belle Starr stood before them, with the shotgun slung across the bend of an arm. The twin muzzles lifted, ready; finger through trigger guard, she glared at these intruders. For what seemed a full half minute they all stood as they were, no one moving. Then, slowly, the shotgun lowered a trifle. Belle's other hand came to rest against her hip. Her cruel mouth quirked humorlessly.

"Well!" Her eyes, settling on Joe's face, were cold with

dislike. "You actually went and broke him loose! I never thought you'd pull it off. I didn't see how you could back up that talk."

He said nothing. It was Bart who demanded abruptly, "Where are the others?"

"What others?"

"Reb, and Vince Choate. I thought they were here."

"Do you see 'em?"

At her tone, Joe saw Bart's look narrow down. "Don't fun with me, Belle! I asked you a fair question. If Reb ain't here, then where is he?"

"That's the last thing I know, or care to know!" she snapped. "Him, or Vince, either. I kicked 'em out."

Despite himself, Joe couldn't keep from blurting, "Reb Beecher? You did *what* to him?"

"Kicked him off the place! And he went, too—like a whupped dog. That's just what he is. The great Reb Beecher; no more fight left in him than a hound with his tail tucked under!"

"Now I know you're lying!" Bart said.

The woman's head whipped around; the shotgun's muzzles lifted slightly. But then she shrugged. "Didn't you tell him, kid?"

Joe felt Bart's questioning stare, and he admitted the truth. "Reb wasn't a hell of a lot like I remembered, come to think of it. Like something had gone out of him. I figured he'd snap out of it, after he got over the shock of what happened on the train job. But—maybe not."

"And that other cur dog. That Vince Choate!" She spat the name as though it tasted bad. "Second time I caught him trying to get my Pearl into the barn, I had all of *him* I was gonna stand for!" She patted the gunstock. "I told him and Reb, both, they could get the hell off my place if they didn't want this thing going off in their faces. Don't think they didn't leave!"

There was a silence. Narrowly, Joe watched his brother and saw Bart absorbing what he'd heard. Bart pushed back his hat, dragged a sleeve down across sweaty, beard-stubbled cheeks. He looked suddenly tired, and his shoulders drooped even more. It suddenly struck Joe that they were both little better than scarecrow figures, filthy from the days of riding.

Bart said, in a quiet voice, "You don't know where they might have gone to? You sure?"

"They never told me," the woman answered crisply. "And I damn well never asked."

Joe looked at his brother. "Guess we might as well be traveling . . ."

"You do that!" Belle Starr moved away from the door, offering them room to go. "And after this do me the favor and just stay clear of Younger's Bend. You'll find no welcome here—you, nor any part of that Beecher crowd. I get enough trouble from Ike Parker's marshals, without letting no out-of-luck bunch like you hang around to Jonah me!" Her hands tightened on the shotgun. "Now—the both of you. Git!"

Bart, pulling his hat again into place, stiffened. Joe held his breath as he saw the shine of anger heating up his eyes; he knew that no one, whether man or woman, had ever ordered Bart Dolan off at the point of a gun—like a tramp, or the whipped dog she had called Reb Beecher. Despite all that had happened, and despite the torment of his hurt, there was spirit in this man even if Reb and Vince Choate had lost theirs.

But then Bart's stubbled cheeks bunched as his jaw clamped hard; he took his eyes from Belle and he strode stiffly out of the cabin. Joe lost no time in following. They went to their horses, swung into saddles without a word and without another look at the homely woman or her gun. Yet Joe knew the weapon would be hung across the crook of her arm and the cruel eyes, under the wing of coarse black hair, would be watching them jog away down off the bench, and turn up the brush-choked canyon trail for the last time.

"That's that!" Joe said. "Where to, now?"

Eyes set straight ahead, the other merely shrugged. He tried again.

"I was thinking, why couldn't we head over to the Cherokee Strip, try to catch on with one of them big cattle outfits? We'd likely be safe enough, and we could put some money in our pockets while we decide what to do next. There's nothing for us hereabouts."

This time Bart looked at him. "You want me to learn to punch cows for twenty a month and found? At my age?"

"A man has to eat."

"I got more to think about than just filling my belly!"

And then the talk suddenly broke off and Bart smoothly slid the gun from his holster, both men drawing rein as they heard movement in the brush above the trail. Something or someone was hurrying through the scrub timber there. Joe, nervously fumbling at the gun shoved behind his belt, searched the thick foliage, caught a glimpse and lost it again, then suddenly exclaimed, "Wait! Hold it, Bart! It's Pearl!"

She came half-running, half-sliding down the bank into the trail; she was panting and disheveled, her cheek smeared with dirt, a twig tangled in her hair. Her breast heaved inside the skimpy cotton dress as she caught at Joe's stirrup and clung while she got her breath.

"What do you want?"

The girl managed to settle her breathing enough to say, "I overheard all that business at the cabin. I had to run wide to keep Maw from catching sight of me. You still want to know where to find Reb Beecher?"

The brothers exchanged a look, and Joe cursed inwardly as he saw Bart's quick interest. Bart demanded, "You know where he is?"

"I reckon. I heard him and Vince talkin', just before they left. And I heard 'em mention the Cave."

"'The Cave'?" Joe asked his brother. "That mean anything to you?"

Bart nodded. "Sounds as likely a place as any. We'll look there."

"But what good will it do? You can't build the gang again. Belle told it right; Reb ain't any more what he used to be, and Choate's no better."

His brother's mouth had settled into uncompromising lines. Stubbornly he said, "They're a start, at least. And they're better than nothing. Hold 'em together long enough for one last job, and that's all I ask."

"Oh, hell!" With a groan, Joe gathered the reins—and felt Pearl's fingers at his stirrup.

"Let me go with you, Joe!"

He stared down. "Let you *what?*"

"Please! I can't stand it here no longer. I—I'll go crazy, I tell you! I just got to get free of that old bitch!"

He said gruffly, "Nothing *I* can do!"

"Aw, please!" She caught at his pantleg. "I won't be no trouble. I—I could be real nice to you, Joe. Don't you like me none?" She turned suddenly coquettish, and put up a hand to do something to her uncombed tangle of hair. "I ain't too bad-lookin' . . ."

Joe felt the tide of warmth into his face. "Good God, Pearl!" he blurted in his shocked embarrassment, and involuntarily gave the reins a jerk that pulled his horse away from the reach of her hands.

But she wasn't through. She turned to the man on the black. "Bart, I done you a favor," she pointed out, the words tumbling over one another. "I told you where to find Reb Beecher. Least you can do is return it." She reached for his arm. "Come on! Have a heart! Take me with you! *Please!*"

Bart shook free. "Get away!" he snarled, and kicked the black forward.

Pearl stumbled and nearly fell. She caught herself, staring after them as their mounts lifted into a canter. "Oh, you bastards!" she whispered. Then she raised it to a shout. "*Bastards!*" And, standing there, she began to cry—despairing and bitter sobs.

They rode on. But Joe Elliott's blood ran cold in his veins, with helpless pity; there was nothing he could have done, yet he knew the sound of that unhappy and ill-fated youngster's weeping, fading slowly as the canyon closed about them, was something he would never lose—however far he might place Younger's Bend behind him.

CHAPTER XIV

The crack of a rifle shot was sudden and startling; the two riders, reflexes dulled by hours in saddle, pulled up their horses and Joe saw Bart Dolan sway unsteadily as the black sidestepped under him. Echoes of the shot bounced off sandstone rock faces, and were sopped up by surrounding masses of pine timber. Then they died and the silence of the hills and the forest settled again, broken by the squawk of a jay somewhere in the trees, the nearby brawling of a mountain stream that flanked the dim trail they had followed during the last slow miles.

Joe Elliott, warned by the burning sensation settling in his chest, knew he was holding onto his breath and slowly released it. He waited, watching his brother.

There was no arguing with him, not any more; Joe had long since given over trying, and had followed the other's lead without comment or question. Bart had set a course south of the Canadian that had brought them, now, some forty miles from Belle's place and deep into the hills, pushing ahead with a doggedness and a stubbornness that seemed incredible from a man so hurt and saddle-weary. Now Joe waited for his brother's decision; and when Bart kicked his tired horse forward again, he followed without comment. But he pulled the six-shooter from behind his belt with his left hand and held it ready, the long barrel resting on his thigh.

The last columns of red-boled pine fell away; and here Bart pulled up again and Joe moved ahead, putting himself at his brother's stirrup. Following the other's searching stare, he saw nothing more than another hill face rising in front of them, with house-sized boulders at its base, and slants of bare sandstone reaching steeply into timber. In the rays of nearing sunset, the whole mass seemed to burn with a blood-red glow.

"Is this what we've been looking for all day?" Joe demanded. "I don't see any cave . . ."

His answer didn't come from Bart. It came in the form of another rifle shot, its point of origin lost somewhere in the jumbled rocks. Joe thought he heard the shriek of the bullet, whipping through pine-tree heads above them. Bart Dolan cursed. And then the outlaw cupped a hand at his mouth and sent an angry shout across the stillness: "Reb! Vince! Whichever one of you it is—cut it out, damn you! This is Bart!"

Silence again, as echoes of the second report bounced away through the hills and were lost. "It might not be either of them," Joe reminded his brother.

"We'll damned well soon find out!" Turned reckless by impatience, Bart kicked the black hard and sent it directly forward. Nothing happened. Joe waited tensely as his brother covered half the distance, then reined in again. "Well?" Bart shouted.

A bodiless voice drifted out to them. "Come ahead!" It was the voice of Reb Beecher.

Seeing the black start forward again, Joe gave his buckskin

a kick. The tired animal tossed its head and carried him out of the timber, brought him even with Bart Dolan just as the latter neared the rocks. There was an opening among the weathered slabs of sandstone, a boulder-strewn and roofless crack that made a natural gateway. As they neared this a shadow detached itself and became Reb Beecher, standing in the opening with a rifle in his hands. He peered at the newcomers with red-rimmed eyes. He seemed even a little shabbier, a little more stooped, in the few days since Joe saw him at Belle's cabin. A stubble of gray whiskers blurred the outlines of seamed and sagging cheeks.

He said, as the riders pulled to a halt, "Be damned if I thought I'd ever see you again, Bart!"

"I got nobody but the kid to thank for it." From the stiffness of this exchange, it was evident they were sparring, neither one quite forgetting what had happened in that woods south of Newton. Bart Dolan was never apt to forgive the man who'd run out on him under the guns of a posse; and Reb Beecher had sense enough to know it.

The old outlaw had barely glanced at Joe. "Glad you made it," he said. "Seen you from the lookout, but had no idea it could be you." He put up a hand to scratch at his stubbled chin, while he studied Bart uneasily from under bushy brows. "How'd you know where to look? Belle told you, I suppose?"

Bart let his mouth quirk with a wicked grin. "Belle told us nothing—except that she'd kicked your tail the hell out of Younger's Bend!" The old man's eyes flicked red angrily but Bart didn't wait for a retort. He straightened in the saddle, looked around. "Who's here with you?"

"Nobody, right now. Vince left yesterday for Poteau—he knows of a couple replacements he thinks he can pick up, for Ordway and Luke Miles. I suppose you knew we'd lost 'em, in that Santa Fe job?"

Bart nodded, his face bleak. "I knew. The old bunch has been whittled down to nothing, just about!"

The old outlaw shrugged—a man who had seen a lot of friends killed, through the years, and could no longer even care. "Put your hosses in the corral," he said. "I'll be at the Cave. We got some grub left, in case you're hungry."

Bart nodded again, and sent the black into the opening with Joe following; Reb Beecher moved aside to make way for them, and they left him standing there.

Beyond the portal, many hoofs had beaten out a narrow and twisting path that threaded its way among the rugged blocks of sandstone. At one point a solid mass had split off to tumble in against the opposing wall, making a low ceiling where a rider had to draw his head down to get clearance. Beyond this Joe Elliott found himself in a steep pocket surrounded by more of the house-tall boulders, with a tree or two growing out of the rocks. They dipped past a shoulder and achieved a larger pocket, formed by sheer walls rising twenty feet or more. And at this point Bart Dolan reined in and dismounted, moving with painful stiffness. "We'll leave 'em here," he said.

Joe could see that this was, in effect, a natural corral. There was only one horse in it just now—Beecher's mouse-colored gelding, nibbling at some wild hay that had been thrown down—but the floor held the droppings of many animals that had been penned here at one time or another. Bart read his brother's look, and nodded. "This place has been used, kid. You might be surprised how much. Even the James boys have been here. Ike Parker's leery of sending his marshals into Choctaw country; but even if he tried it, a handful of men could hold off an army. So, throw off your saddle, kid. We're through running a while."

It was good to contemplate. Joe said as much, and set to work stripping saddle and gear from the buckskin.

Finished, he looked and saw that Bart had uncinched and was trying to lift the heavy tree from his own horse's back. Plainly the wound was giving him a bad time. Without a word Joe stepped over and took the saddle, before the other could let it slide down the black's shoulder and into the dirt. Bart let him have it, and pointed to the spot against one rock wall where he should pile their equipment. Afterward Joe looked around and said, "I still don't see any cave."

"This way."

Bart led him through the maze of boulders and slabs of sandstone. At one point they passed a spring, bubbling out into a natural basin—it seemed that nature had provided this hideout with everything a besieged man could want. Afterward they climbed a narrow crack with steep, high walls, that took them back and up the face of the hill; and here, they found the Cave.

It was hardly more than a shallow trough, under a roof slab of the red sandstone. It seemed to funnel back to nothing, at the cavern's rear, but there was a fair amount of room beneath the overhang. A smell of woodsmoke laced the pine-scented air. Sunset filled the whole cavern with a glow like red fire.

Stumbling up the last steep pitch to the cave opening, they saw Reb Beecher replacing a blackened coffeepot in a bed of coals and ashes. He straightened, tin cup in one hand; his rifle leaned against the slant of rock at his side.

The old outlaw indicated the coffeepot. "Help yourselves."

Bart was breathing heavily from his climb; he let himself down to a sitting posture and leaned his head against the rock while Joe, without waiting to be asked, got two more cups from a small stack beside the fire, filled them both, and handed one to his brother. The coffee was bitter from repeated brewings. Bart drank it slowly, as though savoring the renewal of strength it gave him.

"Well, now." Old Reb spilled the dregs, dropped his own cup beside the fire. He spit out a few grounds between his yellow teeth and said, "We got a couple hours of daylight yet. If the kid's gonna be with us, reckon he can start by going up and takin' over the lookout, till dusk."

Bart Dolan's head snapped up. "Damn it, he's been in the saddle since daybreak—and a good part of a week, before that. He's due for some rest."

"I don't mind—" Joe quickly started to say, but no one heard him. The look that passed between these two seemed almost to crackle with a sudden charge of tension.

Feet apart, shaggy head thrust forward, old Reb looked down at the seated man; his lips barely moved as he said, "He's got to learn what it means to take orders!" Bart Dolan returned the look, and his face was coldly expressionless. He simply rotated the half-filled cup in his hand, swirling the coffee, while his eyes held the other man. But it was Reb who broke gaze.

You could almost see the resolution break and scatter, and all the stiffening went out of his features. The cheeks sagged, the face became an old man's face. Reb Beecher made an angry gesture, and then he turned and snatched up his rifle, tossed it and caught it by the balance. He swung away and went tramping out of the cavern; the scrape of his boots on rock faded slowly.

Bart looked into his cup, lifted it and drank.

Uncomfortable, Joe cleared his throat. "Wasn't worth starting an argument," he said gruffly.

The other shrugged. "That was no argument. He folded up and walked away."

"What did you think you were doing?" Joe's eyes narrowed. "Testing him? To see if he would?"

Bart shook his head slowly. "He was a man, once. Something more than a man—a goddamned legend! As long as we'd ridden together, Reb Beecher would never have taken off of me what he just now did. But, he'd never have let Belle Starr run him off at the point of a shotgun, either." He scowled, and flung his cup against the rock so that it rattled off with a clang and a spray of spilled coffee. "And, dammit, he'd never have run away and left a friend to face a posse, in that woods south of Newton!"

It was exactly what Joe had been thinking. "Kind of looks like the beating you all took on that last job has woke him up to the fact he's an old man . . ."

"It did something more than that!" Bart said heavily. "I've seen a hell of a lot of old men that never panicked the way he's done. You saw how he was hiding in this cave—like an animal in its hole. Right now he's sitting up there on the lookout watching for enemies, when there aren't any within a hundred miles."

Bart dug in his shirt pocket for the limp sack containing the few remaining shreds of smoking tobacco. He held it in his palm, and the hand trembled. Though he'd won the clash of wills with Reb Beecher, it had taken something out of him. He looked utterly fatigued, his cheeks gray and tightly drawn. Joe stood looking down at him.

"What happens now?"

Bart shook his head. "I'm too beat out to know. There's about one smoke left here. Then I'm going to sleep for maybe twelve hours—and wait to see what Vince Choate brings back with him from Poteau . . ."

CHAPTER XV

Joe Elliott was on the lookout when Choate returned. High on the rocky brow of the mountain, with a morning sun beating down and the timbered hills rolling away into distant August haze, he caught movement on the creek trail and fetched up Reb Beecher's old Civil War spyglass for a closer look. The lens was scratched and the mechanism so hard used it was nearly impossible to bring it into focus; but after some effort and searching, he got the horsemen into the circle of the glass.

There were three of them, threading their way among the pines. The one on the lead made an unmistakable figure—he'd have known Vince Choate's bulky, thick-shouldered shape anywhere. He made another sweep with the glass, discovered nothing more. So he slid the instrument back into its case, and went to tell Reb Beecher his news.

Beecher wasn't in the Cave. Joe stood listening to the utter stillness of the place, stillness broken only by the humming of a fly and by the heavy breathing of Bart Dolan, who had spread a blanket back in the rear of the cavern where the floor was level enough. For some minutes Joe stood and looked at the sleeping figure of his brother, and then turned away without waking him. He walked to the mouth of the Cave and put his shoulder against the grooved trunk of a single big pine tree that stood like a sentinel, seeming to grow out of the naked rock. Presently there was a scraping of boots over rubble and he saw Reb Beecher toiling up the hill toward him, head bent against the climb.

Reb had been down to the spring; he carried his rifle, and a couple of water cans slung across a shoulder by their leather straps. He came on doggedly and, when he reached the cave entrance, unslung the canteens and passed one over to Joe as the latter extended a hand for it. Reb lowered the rifle, leaned his hips against the slanting wall of the trough as he unstoppered and drank from the other can.

Joe washed out his mouth and spat, drank deeply, poured water into a palm and wiped it over his sweating face and around the back of his neck. "There's riders coming," he said then, casually.

Reb jerked the canteen from his lips, water spilling through his gray chin stubble as he stared at the other in alarm. "Riders! Why the hell didn't you say so?" He began hurriedly to screw the cap back onto the mouth of the can, missed the threads on the first try. Joe shook his head.

"Don't get excited. It's only Vince. I saw him through the glass. He has a couple of men with him—the ones he went after, I figure."

"How the hell do you know who he's got with him?" Reb retorted. He dropped the canteen he'd finally managed to stopper, took up the rifle again. "And how do you know they weren't followed? Be a hell of a note if he's gone and led the law in here!"

"Vince Choate has better sense than that, I reckon," Joe said with a shrug. "Anyway, I gave the country a good combing with the glass. I saw nobody on his backtrail."

Beecher stabbed him with a dark, unsatisfied stare. "I'm goin' down to the gate," he said curtly, and hefted the rifle by the balance. "You better get back on that lookout and make sure."

But actually neither of them moved, for over Reb's words had come the first sounds of someone climbing toward them. They stood and watched as Vince Choate came working his way up the steep crevice, with a couple of men behind him. He didn't look up, concentrating instead on the climb—stumbling occasionally and catching his stride again with a swing of heavy shoulders. His companions, from the looks of them, were a nondescript pair of typical Indian Nations toughs.

Reb, still scowling, ground his rifle butt against the rock floor and bent forward a little, leaning on it. "Vince?"

The big man lifted his head now. "Who the hell'd you think it would be?" he yelled back. He paused a moment to scrub a shirtsleeve across broad, sweating cheeks. And then the arm dropped slowly; the eyes in the piggish face settled on the young fellow standing next to Reb Beecher, and Joe saw the hot anger that leaped into his stare.

"So!" he growled. "You come back! I seen my buckskin, that you stole—down there in the corral; looked like you didn't do more'n half-run the guts out of him." His muddy eyes flicked to Joe's waist, to the handle of the gun thrust from behind his belt. "I'll take my gun, too!"

"When I'm ready to give it back," Joe said crisply, and saw those mean eyes narrow. Vince had picked up another revolver somewhere, to fill his scarred belt holster. Joe caught the slight movement of his hand, thought for a moment the big fellow was going to draw on him; but he clamped his jaw and refused to let his own nerves bait him into a foolish move.

Then the tension broke as Reb Beecher spoke up, reverting again to the upsetting fears at work in him. "All that can wait!" he said crisply. "You sure your backtrail was clear when you rode in here, Vince?"

Choate gave the other man an angry look. "You think I was born last week sometime? Hell, I never yet left a trail when I didn't want to be follered. You should ought to know that!"

Reb seemed only partly satisfied. He rubbed a hand across his mouth and looked at the silent pair who stood beside Choate, awaiting their cues. "What have you got here? You told me you were going to get us Chad Galen and Murray Hoyt. I never seen either of these."

His tone pulled Choate's mind off his hatred of Joe, put him on the defensive. "You think you could do better? Galen I couldn't find at all. And Murray Hoyt turned me down. He said he wanted nothing to do with Reb Beecher, or anybody connected with you."

"He said that?" Joe saw how the old outlaw stiffened. Reb's gray head lifted and knots of muscles writhed behind the sunken cheeks. His fists tightened on the rifle barrel. "That dirty bastard!" And Joe shook his head, thinking, Don't you know, even yet? Are you still stuck in the past—and in your own legend?

"Well, anyway, I got you some men," Choate went on, his tone still resentful. "God knows I didn't have time to look very far. But I ran into these two, over toward Poteau, and I figured they'd do for a try. This one's Charlie Crow. I've known him a while—he's a good boy . . ."

Charlie Crow was an Indian, or at any rate a half-breed. He had the cheekbones and the dark skin; and the black hair was worn long and uneven, as though he kept it hacked off with the bowie knife he wore in a belt sheath balancing the worn holster. But he was tall for an Indian, and his eyes were a white man's eyes—not quite blue, not quite hazel. They looked oddly pale against his dark face. He was a young fellow, Joe would estimate. There was an uneasy eagerness to be accepted, in the look that returned Reb Beecher's stare.

Beecher raked the young half-breed with a glance and passed him over. The second one Choate had brought back with him was white, a man of medium size with a heavy fall of reddish mustache over his tight-lipped mouth, and a challenge in the protuberant eyes behind sandy lashes. "Ed Thomas," Choate said by way of introduction. "I took him on Charlie's say-so. Charlie vouches for him."

Beecher considered the redhead, with open suspicion. "Before I take on any man, I got to know something more than that!"

Those other eyes narrowed; the mouth, below the ruddy brush of mustache, drew down hard at the corners. "Like what, for example?"

"I want to know who the hell you are!"

The man's look met his challenge, unwavering. Then, seemingly about to speak, Ed Thomas looked past and beyond the old outlaw and Joe saw the sudden change in him—saw the involuntary stiffening, the slow widening of sandy-fringed eyelids, the unmistakable expression of horror that warped and froze on his face.

In the same breath he heard Bart Dolan's quiet voice, saying, "I can tell you who he is, Reb. His real name is Horn. He's a Pinkerton man . . ."

Unnoticed by anyone, Dolan had moved quietly forward out of the shadow of the cave. He stood bent a little, with a hand against the slanting rock to support him, the other empty at his side. For a moment, there was no sound at all except the buzzing of that single busy fly, just under the rock roof. The accused man seemed wholly incapable of speaking, or moving, or taking his terrified look from Bart Dolan's face.

"A Pinkerton!" Reb Beecher echoed hoarsely. "You know this for a fact?"

Dolan nodded. "He came to that jail up in Kansas to have a look at me, second day I was there. He was making big brags that it was the end of the Reb Beecher outfit—and he was on his way to finish the job . . ."

"No! You got the wrong man!" There were beads of sweat along the line of the Pinkerton man's hair, and his face looked sick. "I don't know anybody named Horn! I—I never seen you before!" But even as he protested, he was making a desperate and hopeless grab at the gun in his holster.

He got a hand on it, but that was all. There was the deafening sound of a six-gun exploding at close quarters; Horn was flung bodily sideward, to strike the slanting wall of red rock. And the gun Vince Choate had drawn roared a second time, spewing white smoke into the motionless air. The second bullet slogged into the detective, slapped his head against the rock with a horrible meaty sound. Slowly, then, the man twisted and rolled down the face of the rock to lie at their feet, torn by the bullets. His shirt was scorched black by muzzle flash at close quarters.

Choate's face was scowling and ugly. "Try to take me in, would he?" he gritted harshly, into the returning stillness that settled on ears ringing with the double concussion. His head turned, then, and he looked at Charlie Crow.

Shocked by the cold-blooded killing, Joe Elliott lifted his eyes and found they were all watching the half-breed Indian, with a dangerous intensity. The fellow had courage—give him that. His pale eyes showed his fright, and his lips held a slight trembling; but he looked straight back at Choate and at the smoking gun. He made no move to touch a weapon of his own. His voice was steady as he said, "Shoot and be damned to you! I never knew he was a Pinkerton spy. He fooled me as much as any of you!"

Vince Choate's gunmuzzle was leveled at the man's belly. He said through set teeth, "Damn you, you sold us out!"

"No," Charlie Crow insisted, but he spoke like a man who knew he was doomed.

Then Bart Dolan said, "Vince, put it away."

The big man turned his head, slowly, and laid his scowl on Dolan. "Do what?"

"Put the gun away. I know Charlie; I say he's telling the truth."

"He's lyin' in his teeth! And, by God, nobody makes a fool of Vince Choate—not more'n once, they don't!"

Bart Dolan hadn't moved. He steadied himself against the slanting rock, head lowered, and speared Choate with a piercing stare. "I said, I vouch for Charlie Crow! Use your head, will you? This outfit needs every man it can lay hands on; we can't afford to go throwing away any that's still willing to ride with us!"

The sense of his argument must have broken through to Choate, finally; the man still scowled, but his eyes fell before Bart's. He looked down at the gun fisted in his hard paw, as though he suddenly didn't quite know what to do with it; and then Reb Beecher settled the matter, with a sigh and a wag of his grizzled head.

"Bart makes sense to me," the old outlaw said. "I'll take his opinion on this man," he added, looking at the half-breed. "I reckon Charlie Crow knows now we got our eyes on him. And he just seen what could happen to him if he takes even a single step out of line!"

A faintest ripple of emotion moved across the face of the half-breed—an easing of tension. But he had the wisdom to keep his mouth shut; his pale eyes held Choate's in a waiting silence until Vince Choate, with a grimace, twirled his gun and rammed it roughly into the holster. "Don't worry," he muttered darkly, "I'll be watching him!"

"All right!" said Reb Beecher gruffly, as though this settled matters. He looked at the body of the dead man, touched the grisly thing with a boot toe so that it gave limply and the head rolled sightlessly. "We got to get rid of this. We can only hope the Pinks don't manage to trace him." He looked at Elliott. "You and Charlie Crow take him down into the trees and bury him."

Joe nodded, his mouth tight shut. Somehow he had been figuring this would turn out to be his job.

CHAPTER XVI

Vince Choate scraped up the last spoonful of beans, scowled into his tin plate, and said, "That wasn't enough to keep a man alive."

"It's all you're getting!" Bart Dolan told him from the shadows; and Choate, who had become a man with a perpetual chip on his shoulder, raised his head to favor the other with a long stare. The glow of the fire gave an ugly cast to his battered face, spread his shadow hugely across the Cave's red wall behind him. Joe Elliott, with spoon halfway to lips, lowered it while he shot a quick look around. Charlie Crow's eyes were pale spots in his dark face, watching impassively; old Reb Beecher chewed at a lump of bread as though he had no interest in what was going on among his crew.

Joe suspected that Bart's wound was hurting bad; he'd withdrawn to his blanket in the rear of the cavern, where his face was barely visible as he lay with his back propped against the rock wall. His voice came quietly in the heavy stillness of the night, dark and vast on the rugged hills that lay around them. "You know how we stand for supplies—

and no telling how soon we can get more. I used up the last of my smoking tobacco today." Bart touched the empty shirt pocket. "And just who in this outfit has money to buy food with? Or, anything else?"

No one answered him, for long minutes. Then Joe Elliott, with a strong desire to say something helpful, cleared his throat and ventured, "Ought to be some deer in these hills. I been thinking tomorrow I'd go out and see if I can't scare one up, or a squirrel or something . . ."

With a curse, Vince Choate flung his plate clattering across the rock floor and lumbered to his feet. He stood, arms akimbo, glowering around him. "Animals is what we are—not men! Living in a damned hole, scrounging for the meat to fill our bellies!" He thrust his big hands before him. "I think of all the years, and all the money that's passed through these fingers! And where is it now? Where the hell is any of it?"

Old Reb Beecher's jaw stilled, in the act of chewing. The light of a memory kindled his faded eyes. "Remember the time we took the express office in Junction City? We went on to Chicago afterward and we blew every dime of it, one solid week of women and food and likker like nobody ever seen. We spent that week living it up in the best hotel in town—right under them Yankee marshals' noses. And not a one of 'em ever spotted us!" He began to laugh. His shoulders shook, and the sound that came out of him was so like an old man's senile cackling that Joe Elliott's blood ran cold.

Vince Choate turned on the leader. "A lot of good it does to talk about those days now!" he snorted. "With the law breathing down our necks—and us still licking our wounds from the Santa Fe job! *That's* what you've finally gone and brought us to!"

"I suppose it was me led a Pinkerton spy in here!" old Reb retorted angrily, and for a moment the two of them glared across the flickering fireglow. Joe Elliott was prepared for anything—even to seeing one of them pull a gun and blow the other's head off.

Then Bart Dolan said, "Shut up! Both of you!"

He was on his feet. Joe Elliott didn't know if it was firelight or fever that shone in his eyes—didn't know if he swayed slightly on his feet, or perhaps the wash of shadows over the rock walls gave that impression. But Vince and Reb, at least, seemed to have been jarred out of their argument. They both looked silently at Bart Dolan, and the latter scowled back and said, "What is it you want? You want to see the outfit go to pieces? Right here—tonight—in this stinking cave? Because, it's where you're heading!"

Vince Choate scrubbed a fist across his mouth, his brow heavy. "Nothing goes on forever. Maybe it's time we stopped crowding our luck, before worse happens to us."

"So you want to quit losers! Walk away from the table with empty pockets!"

Reb and Choate shared a glance and looked away again. Charlie Crow sat motionless and stolidly silent, watching without comment.

Vince said gruffly, "We shot our wad on that Santa Fe job. We got chewed to pieces. Where is there to go from here?"

"If you're really asking," Bart said in a tone that brought all their attention to him, "I'm ready to try and tell you."

"Yeah?" Choate sounded harshly skeptical. "You think you got an idea?"

"I've had plenty of time to work at it," Bart reminded them. "I sat in that Kansas jail and I heard the way they talked about us. They said it was the end of the Beecher outfit—it had been shot to doll rags, and what was left would go crawling back to the Nations and like as not never be heard of again. They showed me headlines and front-page stories in all the big Kansas papers, about the passing of the last of the outlaw gangs. The end of an era . . ."

"Hell with the papers!" old Reb cried hoarsely. "Them Yankee editors been countin' me out, for the last twenty years!"

"But this time they really believe it," Bart insisted. "And for once they're so close to right, it gives us a chance like we might never see again.

"What's the last thing anyone's going to expect of this outfit—after the shellacking we just took?" Bart Dolan looked around at his listeners, letting the question soak in; it was only a rhetorical question, and he proceeded to answer it himself: "They'd never believe we could have the guts and the strength to hit them again—right now—while they think we're still lying low, waiting for the smoke to clear. Well, that's exactly what we're going to do!"

Vince Choate stood and stared at Bart through the smoke of the fire. "You sure that bullet didn't hit you in the head?" he demanded harshly. "Anybody in his right mind could see we're in no shape to think about another job, for months to come."

"Why not?" Bart made a gesture that included the whole silent, listening group. "There's just as many here as the day we hit the Santa Fe. We still got guns and horses, and there's still trails leading north into Kansas. My idea is, we pick a place that's never seen us—a place where nobody'll likely expect to. We hit and get out before they know what's happened!"

"Just a minute!" Reb Beecher cut in. "If you're trying to take over the running of this outfit, looks like you've forgotten a few things. Before you can pull a job, in new territory, you got to scout it. And that can't be done in a hurry. *Any* job—it takes months of planning."

"Hell, yes!" Vince Choate echoed, turning away with a scornful swing of his shoulders.

"Not the one I have in mind."

The way Bart said it caught instantly at their attention; it brought Choate slowly around again. And when Bart went down onto his heels, bringing his face directly into the circle of the firelight, even Charlie Crow leaned forward a little to hear what he had to say.

His eyes seeking his brother's face, Bart said, "Your turn, kid. Tell 'em."

Joe stared. "Me? What do you mean? Tell them what?"

"What you were telling me, all the way down from Kansas —everything they need to know about this Union City burg of yours." He lifted a pleased glance to the others. "Talk about scouting a job! He's spent a year there; he knows it all. Any damn' question I could think of to ask him—he's ready with the answers!"

As Joe looked at his brother, too numbed to speak, Vince Choate demanded, "What the hell's at Union City?"

"A bank," Bart told him. "A nice, shiny, brand-new bank! Man named Slaughter built it, Morgan Slaughter. According to Joe, he's about the biggest stockman in western Kansas. Which means the pickings ought to be good. Better than you'll find in the vaults of many of these farming-town banks, just before harvest time."

Joe Elliott drew a long breath, past the knot of hurt and humiliation in his belly. Something very good began to die, in that moment—a kind of warmth and affection that had seemed to be developing between himself and Bart, during their flight southward from Rose Lenson's farm. Their talk had gradually swung away from the problems of the un-certain moment, had come to settle on Joe and his own experiences of the past two years—prison, and then the Quit-mans and his life with them. Bart had seemed really inter-ested; and Joe had warmed to his brother and let himself be drawn out with questions that, as he looked at them now, took on a different meaning.

It wasn't me at all, he thought bitterly. He doesn't give

a damn about me—he was only pumping me, for whatever I could give him!

His chest muscles seemed cramped and he moved his shoulders to ease them. He said heavily, "You ain't forgetting, I also told you the bank sits right across the street from the sheriff's office!"

"Kid, that's exactly what I mean! Learning that sort of thing is why we usually have to spend a week or more smelling out a job." He turned to the others. "I'm telling you, thanks to the kid here I've got the whole layout of that town in my head. Why, I could ride in there tomorrow, and figure every move in advance."

Bart's enthusiasm was beginning to catch fire. Vince Choate had been listening with the air of a man determined to scoff at anything he heard; but now he said, "I've heard of Morgan Slaughter. The bank his money's in should be worth taking a crack at."

Only Reb Beecher sounded dubious. Perhaps he could see Bart Dolan easing the leadership from his failing grasp, and resented it. He shook his head. "Not so goddamn fast, here! I just don't know about this . . ."

"I don't notice you coming up with anything better!" Vince pointed out, with heavy scorn. "Maybe it's about time you were turning loose of the reins."

Doggedly: "A sheriff's office, across the street! I don't like that at all!"

Bart had disposed of all objections, in his own thinking. "We can allow for it," he said patiently. "One man with the horses, two outside to watch for trouble from the law. Two inside to do the job. It should be enough."

"And, afterward?" the old outlaw countered. "Don't fool yourselves! When we leave that town we'll be on the run—in country we never rode before."

"What does that matter?" Bart dropped a hand on Joe Elliott's shoulder and let it rest there as he added, "Since we're going to have a man with us who knows every foot of it!"

Joe felt the hand like a heavy weight, bearing him down to a point that was suddenly unendurable. With an exclamation he came to his feet, shaking free as he swung to face his brother. "You're taking too many things for granted!" he said. "For one, I couldn't ride into that town! I told you, I'm wanted there for assault and robbery. Minute I showed my face, the law would grab me."

Bart shook his head. "No, kid. Believe me! Nobody'll be expecting to see you; and so—they won't. We'll go in, two or three together. You'll be inside the bank before anyone even has time to take a close look. And by then, it won't matter."

His hands were sweating. He rubbed the palms dry against his thighs. All at once he could see that nothing was going to happen to make this any easier for him. What needed saying would have to be said, and it couldn't be put off.

"All right," he said, and tried to watch all of them at once. "If you got to have it straight out—I just ain't in this thing. Do you understand? I ain't taking any part in it. So, quit counting me in!"

A silence greeted his outburst. Bart was the one who said, in a puzzled tone, "What is it with you? Damned if I figured there was any love affair between you and that town. Way you told it, sounded to me like people up there pretty much treated you like dirt!"

"There was a few gave me trouble," he admitted. "On account of my prison record. But, it wasn't everybody; and a few of them—the sheriff, for one—I guess you'd say they tried to be friends, only I didn't give them much of a chance." He shook his head. "But it's not the town, Bart; it's not even this particular job. I don't want a part of any job, at all!"

Vince Choate demanded harshly, "If you ain't here to join up with us, why the hell did you come in the first place?"

"You know why! I came looking for Bart. I was concerned about him—and besides, I was in trouble with the law and couldn't think of any other place to run. So maybe I did have some half-baked notion I might throw in with the outfit again, if you all would have me. I was sore at the world. I hadn't taken time to cool off or think things through. But, now I have."

Choate's mouth pulled down hard; his eyes were mean and angry. "It's just a little late for that!" he said darkly; but Bart Dolan turned on him.

"Leave him alone!" he snapped. "It's his decision and he's got a right to it!" He looked at Joe again; his tone altered. "We could sure use your help, though, kid! Shorthanded the way we are, without you Union City will be twice as tough to crack." He hesitated. "And I guess you know what makes this job important."

Joe knew, well enough. He thought of Rose Lenson, and of how his brother had talked of her—the need and the hope that were at work in him. One last job. . . .

His throat was dry as he read the unspoken plea in Bart's face. For a moment he nearly wavered. But then he shook his head. "Sorry, Bart. If you'd let me know why you were asking those questions about the town and the bank, and all—instead of springing it on me now . . . Well, hell, I could have told you then!"

Vince Choate's mouth was an ugly shape. "Your kid brother don't approve of us, Bart!"

Joe flung out his hands. "My God! It ain't a matter of approving! Don't you understand? I already spent my year in Lansing; I don't figure to do it again. Can't you all see your luck has run out?"

That stung home to old Reb Beecher, still sitting hunched beside the fire. Slowly he lifted his grizzled head, and the glow of the flames shone on the gray bristles that shagged his sunken cheeks. His voice shook with wrath. "Get rid of him, Bart! Get rid of this punk kid! I don't want to hear any more!"

Bart Dolan's chest swelled, his shoulders lifted on a long breath. "I guess you better leave, then," he told his brother heavily. "Take the buckskin and go. Get the hell out of here!"

Joe Elliott blinked. "You mean—now?"

"You heard me!" Bart was suddenly shouting. "Can't you understand English? All right—so you went up to Flint Rock, and pulled me out of a hole and brought me back. But that's over. You've made your pick and we're washed up. How plain do I have to make it?"

Anger stiffened Joe's cheek muscles, tightened his breathing. "I guess you've said it!" he retorted, and his heel scraped on hard rock as he turned sharply.

The noise he made didn't completely cover that other sound, of metal whispering against holster leather. Vince Choate spoke in a voice like a purr. "What he was really saying, kid, was that he wanted you gone before somebody took it in their head to stop you!" The click of a hammer being thumbed back to cock brought Joe's head around, then, and he froze, staring into the black muzzle of the weapon Choate had drawn.

Choate said, "Too late. You ain't going anywhere!"

CHAPTER XVII

The silence was shattered by Bart's roar of fury. "Let him alone, Vince!"

"No! He's with us or he's against us. I'm not giving him the chance to make a deal with his sheriff friend, so that we ride into a trap when we hit Union City. Or maybe even lead Ike Parker's marshals in here on top of us!"

"Why would I do any such thing?" Joe Elliott protested, feeling sweat break coldly upon his body.

Vince Choate's craggy face was an evil shape, above the glimmering gun barrel. "I killed one man today because I believe in making sure . . ."

"For God's sake, Vince!" he heard his own choked voice saying; and then he clamped his jaw until the ache of it nearly forced tears to his eyes. He wasn't going to beg for his life—not from a man like Vince Choate.

Then a flicker of movement and a sound warned Choate and he was turning to meet Bart Dolan's charge. Bart had laid aside his gun and belt, in the hope of better comfort; he didn't let that stop him now. The fire was between them and he waded right through it, a pair of strides that carried him to Choate's side and got his hands on the man's thick wrist before he could pull free.

Choate cursed, jerking against the grip; the cocked gun exploded, a punishing smash of trapped sound, and a bullet scattered sparks as it smashed a burning stick in the fire. And then the big man tore loose and swung a sidearm blow at his opponent, and the heavy gun struck Bart full in the chest and drove him, stumbling, back against the slanting rock that walled the cave.

As he saw the spasm of agony squeezing Bart's haggard face, Joe Elliott gave a shout and started recklessly forward, unmindful of the gun. Unluckily, the startling thunder of the explosion seemed to have jarred old Beecher into motion; he exclaimed something and came blundering to his feet just as Joe moved, and they collided. Beecher went onto his knees and Joe nearly went over him. As he caught his balance he remembered that he had a gun shoved in his own belt— remembered too late, because Choate's weapon was cocked and falling level on him again and he couldn't brave a try to pull that damned gun free.

But now something blurred in reflected firelight, and a yell of pain tore from Vince Choate. He staggered, as numbed fingers opened and let the weapon fall; he stood with his gun wrist clamped in the other hand and stared down at a length of wood from the fire that lay, one end still smoldering, at his feet. And Bart Dolan pushed himself slowly up from where he had knelt to hurl the stick.

Bart's face was ghastly in the fireglow, the labored breath sawing painfully between his lips. He stooped, got Choate's gun and came up with it. "Lift your hands, Vince!" he said in a voice distorted by pain.

Choate raised them both together, chest high, still kneading his hurt wrist. "Damn you, Bart! You could of broke it!"

"I told you to let the kid alone!"

In that moment Joe could think of nothing but the clubbing smash he had seen his brother take across his wounded chest. "Bart! Are you all right?"

Bart turned on him, the captured gun still covering big Choate. He said harshly, "Get out, kid! Take the buckskin and get the hell out of here—before you tear this whole outfit apart. Go on, do you hear?"

Joe stared at him. He swallowed in a tight throat. "You don't really think I'd do what he said? You don't think I'd turn you in?"

Eyes bright with a feverish glow met his own. For a moment Joe thought he was going to get no answer at all. Then, the tight lips lengthened and flattened; the eyes narrowed. "Just don't try it—that's all!" Bart said, in a voice he had never heard before. And then, again: "Get out!"

Joe looked at them all—Reb Beecher on his knees, Choate holding his injured wrist, Bart with the gun in his hand and the look of pain stamped in his wasted features. Only the 'breed, Charlie Crow, sat just as he had been, absolutely unmoved by what had happened.

Joe Elliott turned and plunged away, down the slanting crevice. Something in that last moment, in the sound of his brother's voice, had chilled his blood. The light of the fire faded behind him and there were the stars and a bright disk of moon, nearly as bright as day; before he reached the corral at the foot of the hill he was almost running, stumbling on the uneven going, his footsteps clattering off the rock.

Then he was among the horses, and they stirred uneasily. He found the pile of saddles and gear and threw a tree on the buckskin, working fast. Afterward he stood a minute, hand on the horn, breathing hard as he keened the stillness but still hearing no sound from up at the Cave. No pursuit—not yet, at least.

But the pressures were on him as he hauled himself into

the saddle. The buckskin sensed his anxieties; he had to speak to settle it. Then he was making his way through the narrow maze of tumbled rock and, riding out through the entrance, put the rocks behind him. The pines at last closed their protective canopy overhead.

A rumor of horses moving through midmorning quiet brought Joe Elliott to his feet, forgetting his gnawing hunger and the restless, troubled night he had spent. He grabbed the buckskin's trailing reins and stood listening, thinking for a moment that the search and pursuit had finally begun—it had been folly to have stayed so close, not taking advantage of a head start, and of last night's clear moonlight, to lay distance between himself and the men in the Cave. But the memory of Bart's sick face held him as if on a tether. The brittle threat contained in his brother's last warning didn't matter—it had been the pain talking, and the fever; Bart surely knew better than to believe, even for a minute, the things Choate suggested.

Anyway, Joe Elliott hadn't gone to all the risk of taking Bart away from that Kansas sheriff, and bringing him through enemy territory to the safety of the Nations, only to turn his back on him now because of a difference of opinion. It would always have haunted him, to think of Bart wounded and probably never knowing if he recovered.

So he stood now in this pine thicket, on a hillside overlooking the trail along the Fourche Moline, and watched in growing consternation as a file of horsemen passed through the pattern of morning sunlight and pine-branch shadows below him. Flashes of light beating off the water made him squint, drawing up the muscles of his cheeks. His fingers tightened on the buckskin's reins.

Vince Choate led the way, his big shape foreshortened by the watcher's angle of sight. The others followed in order —Reb Beecher and Bart, with Charlie Crow at the rear leading an extra horse that must have belonged to the dead Pinkerton spy. It carried a tarp-covered pack apparently containing the gang's slender store of supplies.

The Reb Beecher outfit—what remained of it—was on the move. Appalling enough, was the sight of Bart Dolan once more in saddle when every jar of a horse's hoofs must make it an effort of will to stay there. Much worse was the cold shock that hit Joe Elliott, as he asked himself where they could be headed—and thought of only one answer.

Surely it couldn't be that! Under strength, lacking the man they might have counted on to serve them as a guide, knowing only as much about the town of Union City as they had been able to pump out of him last night—they wouldn't be desperate or mad enough to go ahead and attempt the play Bart Dolan had argued for? But even as he recoiled from the thought, he realized they really *were* that desperate—and perhaps not quite sane—from the frustrations and defeats that had come to plague them. They had nothing else, no other prospects; and what Joe had told them of Morgan Slaughter's bank would have made it a glittering prize, worth just about any risk.

He groaned, and the muscles of his cheeks ached as his jaws ground together. He didn't even see how Bart could last out a trek like the one to Union City, Kansas.

Joe shook his head and turned to the buckskin. He had come to look on the horse as a friend; he laid a hand on its neck and said, in a tone of apology, "Sorry, boy. We got another ride ahead of us. I have to keep an eye on him. You see that, don't you? Why, hell! It wouldn't bother them other three if he was to keel over dead, right out of the saddle!" He looked at the cinch, and then swung astride. "So we'll just sort of tag along—but we'll keep out of sight."

There was no hurry. With Bart in that shape they weren't apt to be traveling fast—it was a long way to where they were going.

But he would always wonder where Bart found his strength and his raw courage. The gang made him no concessions at all, nor did he appear to ask for any; they kept pushing steadily north and west at such a dogged, unrelenting pace that Joe himself would have been ready to ask for mercy if he could. There was never any doubt that he'd guessed right as to where they were headed. They set a course straight toward Union City, and though he who knew the country might have cut off some miles, he stayed behind —he wanted to be on hand if his brother should overextend himself and need him, for any reason.

It was an exasperating business. He had to keep well back, close enough so that he had an occasional glimpse of the men he was trailing, but careful not to skyline himself for them—all too easy to do, on that open prairie.

On the last night, he picketed the buckskin and moved up so close that he could actually see the glow of the gang's campfire. He got down on his belly and crawled, finally bringing up under the cover of a brush clump where he could lie flat and look down on the outlaws' camp, some dozen yards away from him along the floor of the wash. The smell of coffee and food cooking hit him hard, reminded him that eating had been a chancy business ever since that last evening in the Cave.

A lazy murmur of talk reached him on the slight breeze; he saw dark figures moving about, and the clot of horses, and thought he could distinguish Bart Dolan seated motionless by the fire—like a man too exhausted to move. He wished he could hear what they were saying, but he didn't dare try to get closer: This deep in enemy country, nerves would be taut and hands ready to grab for weapons at the first suspicious sound. Finally, seeing no point in running useless risks, Joe withdrew as cautiously as he'd approached. When he deemed it safe, he got to his feet and returned on foot to his waiting mount, and stood with a hand on its neck while he fought out a silent debate with himself.

They're really going through with it! They'll hit town sometime around noon, most likely, and then they'll try to take the bank—just the four of them.

Nothing I can do about it. I don't dare set foot in that town!

But you're the only person in the world knows what's going to happen tomorrow. You can't just stand by.

How can I take sides—either way? I told Bart and the rest I wouldn't have any part of this job. But it doesn't mean I could sell them out to the law, for God's sake! I'm not going to get involved.

Any man who knows of a contemplated crime is involved, morally, whether he aims to be or not. . . .

If it comes to that, where does my loyalty belong? To people like old man Slaughter and Abel Quitman, with all that money in the vault? To the law, that's put its brand on me for something I never did? Or to Bart—my own kin, for God's sake!

Whatever you owed Bart was squared at Flint Rock. Nobody could do anything for him now. He's gone completely out of his head—they all have, to try this with only four men.

So then it's bound to fail, whether I lift a hand or not.

Maybe. But some good men can get killed, men that never hurt you any. And Sid Davis, who'd have liked to be your friend even if he was the sheriff, even if he did have to try and arrest you for what somebody else did to that no-good Rick Slaughter. . . .

Oh, God damn it! Joe Elliott clenched a fist and slammed it against the saddle horn, trying to still the hopeless swirl of argument. The buckskin grunted and shifted its hoofs. "Easy!" he muttered, under his breath. He took the stirrup then and swung tiredly up, feeling every mile he'd covered since that night when he left Quitman's on the run.

He kicked the buckskin and reluctantly it started forward. No need to hang back any longer. He made a wide swing of that draw where Bart and the rest were camped, and pushed ahead with white moonlight paling the stars and smoothing the rough contours of flat Kansas earth.

He was no nearer a solution of his muddled problems when, toward midnight and almost in sight of the lights of Union City, he at last unsaddled and rolled in his blanket for a restless attempt at sleep. He was no nearer when, in gray dawn, he rose and tightened his belt on an empty belly, and prepared to move forward into this day whose outcome lay in a fearful fog of doubt.

CHAPTER XVIII

Joe Elliott sat and looked for a long time at the town, seeing the lifting smoke of breakfast fires and such first stirrings of life as were visible from his cautious vantage point, a half mile out along the south road. Since he had only been gone a matter of a couple weeks or so, he could hardly expect Union City to be greatly changed; yet he felt like a wanderer returned, and he was vaguely surprised to find everything looked just as it had when he left it.

He gnawed at his lower lip. Given the distance, and their probable rate of travel, he had estimated Reb Beecher and the gang could hardly reach here much before noon. That gave him several hours yet. Time enough to do whatever he was going to; time at least to think—as if more thinking was apt to accomplish anything. Well, however he finally decided the big problem, there was one other thing he knew he was determined on, even though he couldn't say when he'd made up his mind.

He spoke to the buckskin, turned it into a hooftrack that angled northwest across the brown prairie and would, he knew, take him at a safe distance past the town. But he rode with increasing caution, and with the naked feeling of traveling—in broad daylight now—through country where anyone he passed would be almost sure to know him by sight, and to know the law was looking for him.

This day that was starting promised to be another in the unending procession of pitiless August scorchers; the sun, climbing, was already beginning to put its hammer blows on the baked land, while the sky turned colorless with heat haze. Joe could feel sweat springing from a body that seemed almost dehydrated, turned to whang leather by the heat and searing wind of days that had gone before.

If the wind was a parching torment, it at least kept a windmill turning. When he came in sight of the farm, the blades of Abel Quitman's mill were a bright, whirring smear of light that made him squint. He pulled up and sat looking over the homely and thoroughly familiar scene, with a rush of affection that it had never inspired in him before: the truck garden where he had labored so many hours, the new barn, the broken-backed sodhouse with the single big sunflower growing out of its roof.

At first he could see no movement except over in the turkey pen. But now the screen door opened and Mary Quitman came out, carrying a pail; at sight of her something squeezed tight in him and stopped his breath.

She didn't notice him. She went directly to the windmill where she hung her pail on the pump's spout, under the silver stream of water, and then stood with the wind pressing against her, molding the long skirt to her body. His eyes full of her, Joe swung down and began to walk forward leading his horse, and the sound of the mill covered his approach.

Mary lifted the bucket off the spout. He said, "I'll carry that for you," and saw her back stiffen. Very slowly, she came around.

An exclamation broke from her lips. The bucket fell, spilling its contents, as she lifted both hands to cheeks gone suddenly white. "Joe! But, you can't be here! After all this time—we thought you must be miles away!"

"I was," he said briefly, looking about. "Where's your uncle?"

Her voice was dull, her still expression heavy with shock. "Not here. He went over to Franklin's, first thing this morning—there's a milk cow he's thinking of buying. He expected to be gone till afternoon."

"Good!" He was instantly relieved to know this. He picked up the pail she had dropped, rinsed it out and refilled it from the spout. Mary watched in silence, then turned and went ahead to open the screen door for him.

Evidently she had been up early, getting ready to start the week's baking before the day had time to get any hotter. Thick sod walls, smoothed off with the hoe and whitewashed, usually managed to keep the house cooler than the sun-shimmering world outside, but now the oven was heating and the clean, yeasty smell of the dough was everywhere. It hit his empty stomach with a solid reminder of the meals he had missed. And Mary must have read this in his face; for, as he placed the bucket on the oilcloth-covered sideboard where the loaves were rising in the pans, she asked quickly, "Are you hungry?"

"I won't deny it."

"Sit down. I'll get you something."

No more questions, he noticed, after the first startled outburst; but her cheeks still held their pallor. As she set about putting together a hasty breakfast, the blue eyes in her fine-boned, almost delicate face kept returning to him. He knew she was anxiously awaiting whatever he might be willing to tell her.

He slacked into one of the chairs at the table, dropped his hat onto the floor beside it and ran stubby fingers through tangled, sweat-matted hair. Suddenly it came crushing home to him—sitting here, in this neat and quiet kitchen—what a sorry, dirty figure he was. And how hopelessly exhausted. It made him apologetic as he said, "I had no business coming here like this, Mary. I wouldn't want to make any trouble . . ."

She had coffee on, and now was slicing leftover potatoes and boiled ham together into a frying pan. "You'll make no trouble," she said.

"The sheriff—?"

"Oh, he hasn't been around since—since that night you left. I'm sure he'd never think to look here for you again."

"But he's still looking? Nothing's changed?" Joe took a long breath. "I guess it was too much to hope for.

"I've thought so many times," he went on slowly, "how different things could have been. If I'd only managed to get to Sid Davis that night, the way I wanted to, and explain about the run in I'd had with Rick Slaughter—maybe it would have been easier to convince somebody it wasn't me that laid for him and robbed him, afterward. Davis might have even gone looking for that fellow, Lamb, while there was a chance of finding him. I wouldn't have had to jump parole—nothing would have to be the way it is . . ."

His voice trailed off as he saw the look on Mary's face. She had turned from the stove, fork in hand, and was staring at him in such a way that he demanded, "Why, what's the matter?"

"What you just said," she answered, still with that odd expression. "I don't understand! The name you used—Lamb? Who was that?"

"Cattle buyer. He was in Huck Kallen's that night, playing poker with Rick, and lost his roll. He stormed out of the place, mad; and I've always figured he's the most likely one to have waylaid Slaughter and took it back again. But, if it was, he must have got clean away without anybody but me suspicioning him."

144

"Then," Mary said slowly, "you *didn't* do it?"

Hurt, he retorted, "Did you suppose, even for a minute, I had?"

"But—you were seen!"

"That's impossible! Who saw me?"

"Why—Rick Slaughter did. He's told everyone he had a clear look at your face, just before you hit him!"

"It's a lie!" Joe exclaimed, brought to his feet. "Unless he just saw what he *wanted* to see! It was dark, that night. Maybe he got a glimpse of somebody's face—and because I'd made a fool of him, in front of the crowd at Kallen's, he convinced himself the face was mine."

"But Tod Grandy says the same thing. He was looking for Rick and he saw you run across the light of a window . . ."

Joe could only shake his head, in bewilderment and the beginning of cold anger. "I swear they're both lying! You've got to believe me!"

Quickly Mary came to him and seized his arms at the elbow, looking earnestly up into his face. "If you say so, of course I believe you—and, I'm glad! I'm glad you didn't do it, Joe. And yet it didn't really matter. Not to me! It wouldn't have mattered, anything they said you'd done!"

And then, as though abashed at what she'd said, she dropped her arms and drew back; but he fumbled and trapped her hands in his, and held her so that she couldn't escape. His eyes searched hers. "Do you mean that? I've honestly never known, with you! Just when I was beginning to think you liked me, you'd turn away. That last night— you came to the barn, and you kissed me; and then suddenly you pushed me off like—like you were scared even to have me touch you! Mary, how could you treat me so?"

"Do you think it was easy?" Suddenly her soft mouth was trembling and there was a shine of tears in her eyes. "Don't you know what would have happened, any time Uncle Abel got even the least hint of the way we—the way I felt about you? It's all the excuse he would have needed to send you away—right straight back to Lansing! Can't you see, I didn't dare say or do anything to give him that chance!"

"Then I wasn't wrong? You really do—?"

Next moment, every bit of her shyness and timidity was forgotten. She was in his arms. The warm pressure of her lips told him that she had wanted this moment as much as ever he had done.

"Oh, I do love you, Joe!" she said, her breath warm against his mouth. "I love you so much!"

"Yeah . . ." Slowly, as though a bright light had been turned off in a cold room, he found himself waking from a dream to drab reality. He took his hands away, and released himself from the tight grip of her arms around his neck. "I'll never forget you said it," he told her heavily. "It's the nicest thing I ever had happen to me.

"And now, I think I better be getting out of here!"

She looked bewildered; her mouth still held the shape of their kiss. She shook her head and pushed back the hair from her forehead. "But, why? You haven't eaten!"

Joe leaned and picked up the shapeless hat he'd placed on the floor by his chair. He held it in both hands, and as he answered her he slowly twisted it out of shape. "Since I saw you," he said bleakly, "I've been with my brother. I met a woman he's in love with. He wants to marry her and I told him he was crazy—I told him an outlaw has nothing to offer a decent woman." He swallowed. "I'd be less than a man if I can't take my own advice!"

"Don't speak of yourself as a criminal!" she cried. "Just because you made one mistake!"

"Believe me! I'd go back to Lansing right now and finish serving out my time for that bank job, if that would settle it—and if I knew there'd be someone like you waiting on the outside. But it's too late! There's this other count against me, now. If I let them take me, on Rick Slaughter and

Grandy's evidence, you can bet old man Slaughter will throw the book at me. Add jumping parole to that—and maybe, too, they find out about something I did last week, over near Flint Rock—" He shook his head. "No, Mary. Every step I take I get in deeper; I'll never get it all straightened out. I'm nobody for you to care about!"

"You mustn't say that!" Her arms were around his waist, her head buried against the front of his sweaty shirt. "I could never care for anybody else. I know it!"

"Oh, Mary—" Hoarsely.

And then they broke apart, as they heard the screen door jangle open.

Somehow, caught up in the intensity of their emotions, they had missed the sounds of a buggy pulling into the yard, of footsteps approaching over the dooryard dust. For the moment, like guilty children, they could only stare at Abel Quitman in the doorway, and meet the heavy-lidded look of his pale and cavernous eyes.

Joe Elliott, who was not a small man himself, had to tilt his head a trifle to meet Quitman's stare. In black jackboots and denims and sweat-darkened khaki shirt, the old man stood and looked at him down that great beak of a nose. At the end of one long arm, pointed to the floor, was the awkward and long-barreled Colt revolver that Quitman always kept, as a precaution, under the seat of the buggy.

"I see," he murmured, looking from Joe to the girl. The chopped-off fan of dirty gray whiskers brushed his chest; his cheeks gathered shadow and the corners of his mouth pulled down. He told his niece, "When I saw a strange horse in the yard, I wondered who you were entertaining while my back was turned. I never expected to find *this*. Or to find you in his arms!"

"Let her alone, Quitman!" Joe exclaimed fiercely. "She's done nothing wrong. Ain't it enough that you've got me?"

"Yes—I have, haven't I?" Cold blue eyes flickered behind their lids and the heavy six-shooter lifted. "The man I took into my house—like a viper, to my bosom! I actually believed, for a while, the influence of a Christian home and clean, hard work might have some good effect on you. What you did two weeks ago proved how mistaken I was. But at least I can rectify my error."

Mary Quitman, always silenced by her fear of this malevolent tyrant, found courage to speak up to him: "Uncle Abel, he says he didn't do it! He didn't attack Rick Slaughter, or take his money!"

"Of course he says that," the old man retorted, scornfully. "And of course you believe him!" He cut his stare again to Joe Elliott, and the gun waggled in his powerful, bony hand. "All right, young man. We'll be going now."

"Where?" the girl demanded, her voice rising. "Going where?"

"To the sheriff."

She clutched Joe's arm, as though to hold and defend him. "No! It isn't fair! You owe him better than that. All the months he worked for you—worked hard—and you paid him less than half what he was worth, because you knew he couldn't ask for more. Now, to treat him like this— I'd be ashamed. *Ashamed!*"

The blue eyes kindled to a fierce light. The gaunt face took on a cast of utter fury and old Quitman moved a step toward the girl with a callused palm lifted. Joe felt certain he was about to strike this niece of his, who had never dared to raise her voice to him before; quickly he moved to put her behind him. "It's all right, Quitman," he said hoarsely. "Let her alone. I'll go with you."

Quitman halted, but his eyes burned with their cold rage. "So this is how you've corrupted her! Her that was given moral raising . . . From knowing you she's lost all sense of honor, of respect for the law or even common decency.

Well—we'll be rid of *you;* and then I can do what's needed to bring her back into the proper way."

Joe saw the girl cringe, and her fear of her uncle hurt him and made him groan inwardly. But he clamped his jaw tight, seeing that anything he might say would only make matters worse for her. He pulled his hat on, dragging it down with a savage tug. Abel Quitman nodded in satisfaction. "Just walk out ahead of me," he said. "And don't think I won't be watching every move you make. I'll have no mercy for such as you."

"I was only fixing him some breakfast," Mary protested, and her voice broke. "Can't you even let him eat it?"

"There'll be food for him in jail," her uncle said crisply. "He's eaten his last meal at *my* expense."

Joe gave the girl a last look, trying to thank and comfort her with his eyes. Her own face looked stricken; she shook her head and reached toward him blindly. He heeled around, then, and walked past Abel Quitman and into the blinding morning sun.

CHAPTER XIX

The buckskin stood where Joe had left it, ground-hitched, near the well. When he started toward it, a sharp command from Abel Quitman halted him. "Leave the horse. I'm keeping it—to replace the one you stole from me when you left."

Joe turned on him. "I never stole anything from you! That old roan was mine, and you know it as well as I do! We had an agreement—he was mine in payment for wages I never got."

"I remember no agreement," the old man replied crisply. "No doubt the buckskin's stolen, too; but I suppose I can't afford to ask too many questions. Mary can put him in the barn." He gestured toward the buggy. "We'll ride in this."

Joe could do no more than stare. "Why, you damned hypocrite! You even had *me* fooled, with your pious talk and your Bible-thumping—and yet you can't even keep a promise!"

The mouth pulled down hard. "Get in the buggy!"

Quitman settled himself with the revolver laid across his knees, one rawboned hand resting on the wooden butt. "You will drive," he said, and Joe took the leathers in silence.

He didn't need any warning or threat, or anything more than the stern and stony look on the face beside him, to tell him he would regret a foolish move. He glanced at the house and saw Mary standing in the door with one hand against the side of the warped cottonwood frame; she looked white and sick. Grimly he slapped the reins against the back of the shaft horse and the animal grunted and started away. Joe turned him into the town road.

Minutes passed in silence. There would be no pleading with this man, even if pride would have let him try; after a year, Joe knew him well enough at least to know that. But he remembered the terrible look of the old man when Mary had dared to beg mercy on his behalf, and finally it prompted him to speak—breaking the silence for the only time: "Don't take it out on her, Quitman! She hasn't done anything wrong."

"I'm very apt to believe that," the old man said coldly. "After what I just saw with my own eyes! I can imagine what must have gone on behind my back, all during those months."

Joe felt his cheeks grow warm with anger. "By God, it's not true! I reckon you could never believe anything decent of *me*—but, she's your own niece! You ought to know she's a decent girl."

"She's a child. If she deserves to be punished, it is my duty to punish her."

"Don't be too sure of that! In case you've lost count, she's eighteen now. She's of age—and one of these days, if you don't watch your step, she's going to forget how scared of you she's always been, and tell you to go to hell!"

"I want no advice from you," Abel Quitman said sharply. Another sidelong glance at the chill, hooded eyes, and at the knuckles squeezed white on the handle of the old gun, warned Joe he might as well save his breath. Better to spend it talking to the sheriff—or to a stone wall!—than on this pious fraud who sat beside him.

The sun stood at high noon as the old buggy finally rolled into town—Joe thought he could have fried an egg on the black leather top, inches above his head. There was more activity than he would have expected, on the street and under the shade of sidewalk awnings; and he remembered then that it was Saturday.

Quitman and his dusty vehicle were such a familiar sight that no one gave them so much as a close glance. On orders Joe drove directly to the jail, got down there and hooked the weight strap in place. By then Quitman had climbed out and was waiting with gun in hand, the brim of his hat throwing its deep shadow across his face. The old man waggled the gun barrel.

"In," he commanded sharply.

Joe eyed the gun. He could feel the sweat running on his body; this near to the moment when the door of freedom would slam shut on him, the urge to rebel ran high. But if he tried a break he had no doubt that the old man would use that gun. So, letting the trapped breath run out of him in a long sigh, he turned and marched into the jail with Quitman close behind him; and in all this time no one had recognized or even seemed to have noticed him.

Thank God, at least it was cool in here—a low-ceilinged, stone building, the bars at the broad-silled windows seemingly strong enough to keep the egg-frying heat of the day from creeping in. Sid Davis was standing before a wooden file cabinet, fumbling through some old correspondence. He half-turned as they entered. He was a man of considerable self-composure, but his responses were not swift enough for this moment. His head jerked and he frankly stared, through steel-rimmed spectacles, until Abel Quitman said, with a scowl, "Well, I've brought you a prisoner, Davis. Do you want him or not?"

That jarred the lawman into mobility. He slammed the file closed. "Hell, yes, I want him!" he exclaimed a little hoarsely. "But I'm damn' well surprised to see him again!" As though he still didn't half-believe it, he walked up to Joe and, with hands on hips, looked him over from head to foot. "You look like you lost about twenty pounds," he said at last, "since that night we sat and talked, young fellow." He glanced at Quitman, not missing the hogleg revolver.

"Where the hell'd you pick him up? At your place?"

Quitman only nodded. The lawman's eyes narrowed shrewdly. "He came back, maybe, thinking because of past associations you wouldn't be apt to run him in . . ."

The old man stiffened; his head pulled up with an expression of stern indignation. "He had no reason to think so! I'm a God-fearing man, Davis. No one should expect I'd let any such considerations stand in the way of doing my proper duty!"

Sid Davis looked at him for a moment; then he nodded, his face expressionless. "No. No, Abel, I guess they shouldn't . . . Well, was there something more I can do for you?"

"No," Quitman said. "I've fulfilled my responsibilities, by bringing him in to you. As a result I've already lost an hour out of the day's work. I turn him over to you—and I wash my hands of him!"

"All right," the sheriff answered, a little tartly. "You just put it out of your mind. Go on about your business. Everything will be taken care of . . . Morning, Abel."

There was a silence, after that, in which they could hear the grind of Quitman's buggy tires mingle with the other street noises as the old man drove away. Sheriff and prisoner stood and looked at each other; and in the door to the cell-block, the stoop-shouldered old man who served Davis as a turnkey stood staring, holding the mop with which he had been swabbing out the cells; the sour smell of disinfectant worked at Joe's nostrils, reminding him of what awaited him.

The sheriff took a breath. He motioned his prisoner to a chair but Joe remained where he was, hat in hand. Davis walked around him to the street door, took a look outside, and then swung the steel-enforced planking shut and snapped the bolt home. A meaningful glance at the jailer sent the latter back to his work.

Seeming to remember, then, that as a lawman with a prisoner he should be armed, Davis stepped and took a scuffed shellbelt and holstered gun down from a wall peg and buckled them around his hips. Settling them there, he walked to the desk and got his pipe from the rack and hung it between his teeth without lighting it. He dropped into his chair and looked up at Joe through the steel-rimmed spectacles, lips pursed around pipestem.

The weight of his stare was hard to endure but Joe stood and waited it out, unmoving, though the cold trickle of a bead of sweat breaking and running down his ribs made him want to squirm.

"I hope you know I'm not happy to see you again," the sheriff said finally, taking the pipe from between his teeth. "I recall you don't like sermons, so I won't make one. But, by God! Anyone who'd go and let himself get caught, after the clear break it looked like you had made for yourself—!" He shook his head. "Ain't you got any better sense than to come back and walk right into Quitman's hands? Did you maybe think he wouldn't bring you in? Or, what?"

Joe's lips barely moved as he said tightly, "Just cut it out, Sheriff. Stop rubbing it in!"

Those other eyes studied him. "I'd have sworn you were long gone from these parts. Two weeks, it's been. Nearer three. And what with the pressure old man Slaughter's been putting on this office, I'm damned if there's many stones I didn't turn over, looking for you. Where did you go, anyway?"

"It's no good asking me questions. I haven't anything to say. You've got me—isn't that enough to satisfy you?"

"No!"

Sid Davis's fingers tightened angrily on the pipe. "Sermon or not, I got to talk sense to you! You're in a bad spot, boy—a broken parole is nothing anyone can shrug off, even without a new charge of assault and battery. It'd go a lot better for you if you could give me anything at all—any slightest indication that you want to cooperate with the law."

Joe looked at him sullenly. "What, for instance?"

"You could tell me what you did with the money you took off Rick Slaughter."

He clenched his fists. That, again! "I never took anything off him. I never jumped him, either. I never saw him again after our fight at Kallen's, that night. I'm telling the truth!"

The sheriff's brows drew down. "It doesn't gibe with the testimony."

"I can't help it! I'm not going to admit to something I didn't do!"

For a long moment the lawman studied him, softly clicking the bit of his pipe against his teeth. Then, shaking his head as though in exasperation, he dropped the pipe onto the desk and pushed to his feet. He walked to a window and looked out upon the shimmering street with his hands behind him, the back of one slapping into the palm of the other. And Joe, pivoting on his heel, waited in silence.

Slowly, Sid Davis turned back.

"This is a lot to ask a man to believe," he said heavily. "Not that it's hard to see how it could have happened—Rick, and Tod Grandy too, might have been in too damned much of a hurry about making an identification, after the trouble they'd both had with you that night. But it's more than any jury's apt to agree to. Believe me! Any man empaneled in this county would think twice before he stood up and called Morgan Slaughter's son a liar. You know what I mean?"

Joe was ready with a bitterly sarcastic answer, but it was never spoken. For as he looked past the sheriff and into the blast of noonday heat beyond the barred window, he suddenly felt a tightness that lodged itself in his chest, squeezing off his breath; the short hairs along his scalp began prickling in cold apprehension. The rider who had crossed the window just then, moving at a slow walk along the street, went on beyond his range of sight. But there was no mistaking the face he'd been allowed to glimpse, however briefly. It had been the 'breed, Charlie Crow.

"Well?" said the sheriff.

Joe Elliott swallowed. A second horseman rode past the window; this one's face was averted but the big shape of him in the saddle was hardly mistakable: Surely he'd know Vince Choate, any place!

"Are you listening to me?" Sid Davis demanded.

He shook himself a little, cutting his stare back to the lawman. "Yeah," he said, but what he was hearing were the words Davis had spoken a few minutes ago: It'd go a lot better for you if you could give any slightest sign that you want to cooperate. . . .

It was still not too late. All he needed was to speak the words that would give the sheriff warning. A man might buy himself a lot, with what he could tell Sid Davis just then!

Face frozen, mouth clamped tight, he met the lawman's stare and saw him slowly redden with anger. The sheriff made a curt gesture.

"All right, mister!" he snapped. "I'd like to help but you don't make it easy for me. Yeah, I'll check again on Grandy and Slaughter's story, about what happened that night; but it's not apt to do you any good. And right now I got no choice but to lock you up." He lifted his voice to call into the cell block at the rear of the jail. "Harry! Fetch your keys . . ."

The old jailer was just then shuffling in, his mopping finished. He set mop and pail against the wall. He said, "OK, Sid," and took the keyring down from a peg where it hung when not in use; he stood waiting, swinging it in his hand.

The sheriff meanwhile had moved around behind his desk again, where he seated himself and took a large manila envelope from the top drawer. "I reckon you know the routine," he told his prisoner dryly. "Give me the stuff from your pockets."

There was little enough of it—a dirty handkerchief, a cheap claspknife, a few coins. Joe fished them up with numb fingers, his whole attention straining toward the stillness beyond the street door. He watched as Davis made a careful inventory on the back of the envelope. Putting the prisoner's belongings inside, he asked, "You had anything to eat?"

Joe had to stir himself to answer. "What? No—no, I guess I ain't." He had actually almost forgotten. His tone got him a look from the sheriff as Davis tongued the flap of the envelope, pressed it down with a broad thumb.

"I didn't think so—you look half-starved. Well, I guess I can scare up something for you. Come to think of it, I haven't had my own dinner yet." He dropped the envelope back into the drawer and closed it.

"All right," he said, with brusque efficiency, and slid the gun from his belt holster as he got to his feet. He gestured with the barrel, indicating the cellblock door where the jailer stood waiting. "Inside. And don't give me any trouble," he added, as Joe stood motionless. "You're too smart a fellow for that."

Whether or not he really thought he needed to give that warning, he got nothing from the prisoner but an abstracted stare. Then leather squealed on bare floorboards as Joe turned and walked to the cellblock door, and through it.

Harry, moving ahead of him, had the barred door of a cell open and waiting with the key in the lock, ready to turn and close him in. On the threshold, Joe hesitated involuntarily as he saw the hard iron bunk, the slop bucket in the corner, the single tiny window. But he drew a long breath and set one foot inside—just as the first shocking break of gunfire began in the street before the jail.

CHAPTER XX

No one ever knew for certain how the shooting began, that August day—whether some townsman saw something that struck him as wrong, in the activity at the bank, or whether it was one of the outlaws themselves who had a failure of nerve and suddenly began to use his gun. Whoever he was, if the man who fired that first shot was still alive ten minutes later when things were over, he never came forward to make the claim.

Within the jail, the first startled moment found Sid Davis taken wholly by surprise; an isolated gunshot or two was no rarity, on a Saturday noon when some farmhand or puncher in off the prairie might get his weekend drinking started prematurely. But it didn't stop with that first gunshot, or the second or third, as normally should happen. It didn't stop at all. And suddenly a man's voice, with a break of hysteria in it, shouted: "It's *Reb Beecher!*" A second voice took up the cry, and then others—tossing it back and forth, above the growing tumult of exploding gunpowder. And Sid Davis, with a startled oath, whirled and rushed for the street door.

Joe Elliott, turning, saw him fumble the bolt, shove it free and go dashing out of the building, letting the heavy door rebound off the stone wall. The jailer, motionless at Joe's elbow, stood dazed and blinking as time-slowed reflexes refused to function. He gave hardly any resistance when Joe whirled on him, with a thrust that took the barred door out of his hand and staggered him. Seizing the slight frame of the man by both shoulders, Joe swung him into the cell, clanged the door shut on him and turned the key in the smoothly oiled lock. He snatched the keyring free and sent it sailing down the corridor, hearing it clatter against the wall but not bothering to see where it lit.

By then he was already out of the cellblock, hurrying through the sheriff's office to the street door that stood partly open. Out in the street there was a continuous, sporadic gunfire. Just as he reached the door someone went running past it and he ducked back again, pausing to get his bearings.

He could see little, in that first instant, except a boiling of hoof-raised dust. But there could be no doubt of it—Reb Beecher had stuck his head into a hornet's nest! Joe Elliott thought there must be at least a dozen guns trained on that area in front of the bank. He spotted one man at a second-story window, working a rifle. Others hugged the shelter of doorways on either flank of the barnlike building, and others across from it—he got the impression they were trying too hard to stay in cover to be doing much effective shooting.

A lot of shells were being spent, mostly wasted; but the noise was enough to cause a frenzied pitching and squealing of horses struggling to tear loose from their tethers at hitching racks along the street. A few animals—the gang's, probably—were running wildly through the streaking dust, stirrups flopping. One was down; it lay on its side, kicking out its life with aimless threshings, its head lifting and dropping back again, while blood ran to make a widening crimson pool where flies were already gathering.

Not far from the body of the dying horse, Charlie Crow's lifeless shape lay face down, booted legs spread wide and one arm trailing limply across the edge of the sidewalk. Another of the outlaws was putting up a fight from directly behind one closed leaf of the bank's big double door. And out in the open, kneeling on the broad steps—hat gone and the noon-bright sun full upon his graying head and bent shoulders—old Rebel Beecher had the long barrel of a Navy Colt laid across the bend of his left forearm and was firing steadily.

It was a last mad, heroic stand on the old wolf's part, and it was something to see. When a bullet chewed a long, clean sliver from the board under his bent knee he didn't even flinch. He steadied and coolly fired an answering shot, and the recoil bounced the muzzle of his gun high and he brought it down again, with smoke spurting to form a fog about his grizzled head. On the tail of the shot Joe had heard a scream of terror and agony; he looked in time to see a man rise up from behind the watering trough where he had crouched for protection—spring up like a puppet worked by an inexpert hand, arms windmilling grotesquely and the sun smearing on the metal of the gun he flung wildly away.

Despite the sudden smear of blood across his face, Joe knew the man was Tod Grandy. He registered the fact with half of his numbed consciousness, not really feeling anything —not even when he saw the man who had tormented him collapse lifeless against a corner of the trough, and flop down into the mud that overflow had made in the dirt.

Joe Elliott was thinking, in a dazed and inefficient manner. He knew there was a shed behind the jail, where Sid Davis normally kept a couple of horses. He could never hope for a better moment to slip back there, unnoticed in this melee, and get the saddle on one of them, with the hope of putting a lot of distance behind him before his escape was even discovered. The idea actually brushed his mind, but it was gone again and lost while he was scarcely even aware of it. For his real attention was focused on the bank—on Reb Beecher kneeling in the sun before it, and that other gun firing from just within the half-closed doors. He stood unaware of himself and incapable of movement.

And thus he saw Sid Davis step out from under the shadow of a wooden restaurant awning, some dozen yards to his right. The sheriff held a smoking gun. He moved forward into the street, deliberately circling a hitching rack in order to clear the horses that were pawing and rearing and trying to wrench the posts out of the ground. Dangerously close to those wildly lunging hoofs, he stopped and deliberately took aim. He fired just once, and then lowered the gun as though he knew the shot was good.

Yonder, Reb Beecher jerked as though a boot had kicked him in the chest. He toppled slowly onto his side. The gun fell from his hand; he appeared to reach for it, and lost his balance and went rolling down the three wooden steps. When he brought up at the foot of them—a motionless bundle of old clothing, that scarcely looked as though they had a body inside them—anyone who saw must have known that a legend was finished, that a part of the past was over and Rebel Beecher had led his final raid.

Seconds later Joe forgot him, totally, for a bullet had struck the glass of the bank door, knocking it out in a smash of sunlight on splintered shards. It was exactly as though he felt it with his own tensed body. His breath caught, in the concentration of listening for another shot from the gun stationed behind that door; only, the shot didn't come. Instead, just within the opening, something fell in a sprawl and lay motionless. He could see it was the lower half of a man's body—a pair of booted legs. Cramped breath exploded from Joe Elliott's lungs as he heard himself yell his brother's name; and after that, somehow, he was out of the sheriff's doorway and was running, through hot sunlight and streaking dirt and powder stink.

His legs seemed wooden, without feeling. He stumbled on a street rut and almost went sprawling. He didn't even know that guns were still banging and that his own hands were empty. He passed Charlie Crow's lifeless body without so much as a look. He did glance at Reb Beecher but all his thought was for that other man lying, half-visible, beyond the bank's doorway.

He halted then a moment, in bewilderment, for suddenly people were pouring out of that door: wild-eyed and shouting humanity—bank customers, and a teller in armbands and green eyeshade; even a woman with her skirts held high and sobbing with fear as her husband hauled her along by one arm. They leaped and stumbled over the prone figure that half-blocked the entrance, and came plunging down the steps at Joe in a way that bid fair to bowl him over. But he stood his ground and they had to split and pass on either side of him. Someone's shoulder caught him in the chest, staggering him briefly. Then, dimly aware that the last of the shooting had ended, he plowed his way on up the steps and through the door—and stood staring at the man who lay dead there in a pool of his own blood, a six-gun lying beside him.

It wasn't Bart at all. It was Vince Choate.

He was still taking in this fact when the sound of a blow and a scuffling of bootleather brought his head up. The barnlike room could have been deserted, from his first glimpse of it. The teller's cage and the desks beyond the railing were empty. One of the two long tables, where customers stood to fill out their deposit slips, had been overturned and the floor was littered with broken glass and papers and even a scattering of green bills. At the end of the room the shining face of the big steel vault, set in brick and concrete, gleamed through the shadows.

And then Joe saw the men.

Morgan Slaughter had been brought to hands and knees; he crouched there like a hurt animal, his massive, white-maned head hanging. Bart Dolan leaned over him with six-gun clubbed and ready. While Joe stared, Bart seized his prisoner by a fistful of hair and jerked upward, dragging another groan from the banker; Slaughter's head lifted and showed the blood pouring down the side of his face, from a laceration on the forehead.

"Don't think I don't mean it!" Bart told him, in a voice so harsh and savage Joe scarcely recognized it. "The next one will crack your skull like an egg!" He raised the gun barrel. Slaughter eyed it, groggy with pain, but without any shade of fear in him as he answered.

"Go ahead, then, damn you!"

"Open the vault."

"I told you, I can't! It's on a time lock. Now it's been shut, nobody on earth could open it before nine tomorrow morning."

"You're lying!" In a fury of frustration, Bart Dolan shoved the gun muzzle against the side of the prisoner's head with force that made Joe wince.

"If you don't believe me," Morgan Slaughter gritted through bloody lips, "then go ahead and pull the trigger. But you'll hang for it!"

"The hell with that!" Bart said, ignoring him. "*Open that vault!*"

His face, behind a week's growth of beard, was drained white by illness; the eyes seemed to recede deep into his skull. Where he could have found the strength to manhandle someone as big as Morgan Slaughter, Joe failed to imagine. It wasn't a sane strength; the twisted look on Bart's face was that of a man driven beyond the edge of rational intention. In his rage at Slaughter, for slamming the vault door and so frustrating him, he seemed to have lost all sight of other things—of the gunfight in the street, ended now; even of Vince Choate's death and the escape of those Vince had been holding at bay under his gun.

The gun lay near Vince's lifeless fingers, only inches from Joe's shoe. He looked at it, and slowly stooped and picked it up. It still had a couple of bullets in the cylinder. His mouth tightened as he closed his fingers around the rubber butt. He lifted his head, then, and with the weapon leveled he said, in a voice that didn't sound like his own: "Let the man go, Bart. Can't you see he's telling the truth?"

Bart turned. His eyes, behind lank and streaming hair, seemed to search for the voice that had cut in on his mad raving; and Joe tried again, knowing only that he had to make an impression before the hammer dropped on that six-shooter pressed against Morgan Slaughter's head. "Don't you remember, Bart? I told you he had all the newest gadgets. There was bound to be a time lock—and killing him won't open it! You got to let him go!"

His brother looked down again at his prisoner. Suddenly he thrust him away, loosing his grip on the man's hair and letting him drop heavily. For that one moment, Joe thought his argument had actually jarred through. In the next breath he knew he was wrong.

He saw it, in the glittering stare Bart turned on him. "Yeah, you told me," Bart said hoarsely. "And that ain't all you did!" The weapon in Bart's hand turned and the gaping muzzle of it pointed squarely at Joe Elliott's chest. He took a step toward his brother, and then a second; the gun and the furious stare were unwavering. "Vince warned me you'd sell us out. Up to the last, he kept saying we'd find your sheriff friend ready and waiting for us!"

"No!" He tried to shake his head but it wouldn't move; his body felt powerless. "God, no! I had a chance to tell, but I never did—not even to help myself, when they threw me in jail. What you ran into here, just happened. You got to believe me!"

But his protests fell on unhearing ears. All the time he was speaking, Bart kept pacing forward across the litter on the floor. Beyond, Joe could see Morgan Slaughter trying to push himself up, only to fall back onto one elbow with the blood dripping off his cheeks.

"Bart! *Don't!*"

The cry exploded from Joe Elliott and at the same instant he made a senseless try to leap aside, out of the path of the gun. It exploded, with an ear-smashing sound. Something like a red-hot poker slashed across his ribs, spinning him though without force enough to knock him down. He caught himself somehow and then, with an unthought and instinctive move for self-preservation, shoved Vince Choate's rubber-handled Colt in front of him and blindly pulled the trigger.

The second shot slammed into the echoes of the first. Only half-believing, Joe saw his brother halted in midstride as though he had walked into a wall. Bart's head was flung back. He toppled, twisting as he fell—like a cat, trying to land on its feet. But he hit the floor in a loose sprawl; and Joe, taking one look at the gun smoking in his hand, flung it savagely away. It clanged against the front of the teller's cage, bounced off in a spinning smear of metallic light, as he went forward on trembling legs.

He reached his brother and went down on his knees, the weight in his own chest seeming heavier than Bart's wasted frame when he got him by the shoulders and lifted him. The head flopped limply against his arm. "Bart!" he moaned brokenly. "Oh, God! Bart, I'm sorry! I didn't mean to!"

He couldn't bring himself to see what the bullet had done to his brother's chest. Instead he looked into a face that already seemed half-dead, and into eyes that were white half-moons below the fluttering lids. He knew the man was past hearing him. Dumb with grief, he watched Bart's lips stir with the effort of speaking. He bent over him, bringing his ear close, and caught the faintest whisper: "Rose . . ."

The name came out as a long, breathy sigh, and then bright blood began to pour from a corner of Bart's mouth. He choked and coughed on it once, convulsively and feebly; and then he was dead.

Joe knelt there and rocked him gently, unmindful of the blood or of his own hurt, unaware of Morgan Slaughter staring at him or of the men who were cautiously entering the room now—carrying guns, and stepping gingerly over the body of Vince Choate sprawled across the open doorway.

CHAPTER XXI

It was all over, but the excitement still raged. The bodies of Bart Dolan and Vince Choate had been taken outside and laid beside the others on the sidewalk before the bank— their eyes closed, hands crossed on chests and heads propped up so a man with a big box camera could get all four of the dead faces into the pictures he was busily shooting.

Already the confused events of that brief ten minutes were being hardened and firmed into legend. The town had had, at last, its one brief hour of glory. History had begun and ended on this August noon in 1884; in future, Union City would be known solely and simply as the place where Reb Beecher made his last raid. Someday, no doubt, the ladies of the County Historical Society would put up a plaque to mark the spot, with proper ceremonies; and probably on Fourth of Julys young men would re-enact the historic occasion, amid a proper popping of blank cartridges and a clatter of hoofs on asphalt paving.

But no one thought of such things now—least of all Joe Elliott. He sat on the floor of the bank, numb with shock, his whole body burning to the raw disinfectant Doc Reasoner had used in binding up the bullet streak along his ribs. He sat with his back against the wall and legs stretched out before him, listening dully to the activity around him and hardly conscious of the man who had been stationed to guard him.

Other guards had been posted at the bank's two doors, to keep out the excited and curious crowd. A janitor had already started cleaning up some of the mess; Morgan Slaughter, looking deathly pale with a bandage covering his lacerated scalp, had recovered enough to supervise his teller in a hurried count of the money scattered during the abortive raid. This, of course, was the really important business; for the moment, Joe Elliott was virtually forgotten.

But presently Sid Davis came over and stood looking down at him a moment; and a question that been vaguely bothering him made Joe lift his head. "Did anybody think to let Harry out of that cell?" And when the sheriff nodded: "I didn't hurt him any, did I?"

"No."

Suddenly anguish twisted its knife in him and he blurted then: "Sid, what the hell will they do with him?"

The sheriff blinked; his puzzled scowl cleared a little, as he understood. "Oh," he grunted. "I guess now you're talking about that brother of yours. That Bart Dolan." He shrugged. "None of your concern. Whatever's to be done, the county will do it."

"They'll dump him into a hole somewhere—not even mark it decent." Joe's eyes were bitter; his hands clenched until the nails dug into the palms. "It ain't right! He deserves more than that!"

"Since he's dead, the point's hardly worth arguing. I'd suggest you start worrying about your own neck. You were in on this holdup, too, of course?"

"I knew about it. I wasn't in on it."

The lawman eyed him coldly. "Sure! I guess I'm expected to believe that! What the hell else would bring you back here? Or make you come running across the street, into the midst of it all?"

"I could see them dying," Joe answered tonelessly. "I saw Reb Beecher go down. And then I saw somebody in here get it, and I thought it was my brother. All I could think of was, I had to know for sure . . ." Suddenly he felt all the muscles of his face contract and twist into a shape of grief and pain. "And then, by God—I killed him!"

The sheriff's look was noncommittal, his voice gruff. "You want to sit there a little longer? Or are you ready to walk back across the street with me?"

"I can make it."

He hauled himself to his feet—one hand on the wall and the other grabbing the sheriff's arm, while the man with the rifle watched him hawkishly. The bullet-sliced muscles across his ribs stretched and hurt, and he gnawed at a lip while he steadied himself against the pain. "All right," Sid Davis said. "Let's go."

"Just don't rush me!" Joe Elliott protested.

By favoring his hurt side he made it to the door, with the sheriff and the other man flanking him; after the first uneasy step or two he found himself a good deal steadier on his legs than he had expected. He gingerly stepped across the darkening stain of blood where Vince Choate had died. Then the door guard moved aside and they stepped out into the blaze of the sun; and the crowd in the street, turning as the door opened, fell silent to stare at them.

With Davis on one side and the man with the rifle on the other, Joe halted uneasily at the top of the steps. He hadn't known what to look for, but what he saw in the faces below him was an odd blending of hostility and cold curiosity. The sheriff sensed his uncertainty for he said quietly, "It's all right." And lifting his voice, he told the people on the street,

"Stand back, now! Let's everybody mind his own business . . ."

Unerringly, Joe's stare had sought out the place where the bodies of the dead bank robbers were laid out. At once he saw a face he knew, among the men clotted about them; at the same moment someone nudged the big fellow, said something that brought him around to see the group on the bank steps. Rick Slaughter drew himself quickly erect. He gave his trousers a hitch and an expression of wicked satisfaction was spreading his broad lips as he walked over and climbed to face them.

He hung his thumbs in his waist belt; his voice carried loudly in the hush of the street. "So! You came back, did you—and let them take you with your hand in the till!"

"Not so fast, Rick!" Sid Davis said sharply, not wholly keeping the dislike from showing in his voice. "It ain't been proved, yet, that he had any part in the holdup."

"Who you trying to kid?" The man's arrogant face took on a different look, then; his lids with their pale lashes narrowed as he measured the prisoner. "If you really got any doubts—just turn him over to me and I'll beat the truth out of him!"

Stung by this, Joe heard himself saying sharply, "You? You couldn't beat me, the best day you ever lived!"

If he had meant to he couldn't have said anything better calculated to whip the big man into a fury. The licking he took off Joe Elliott in Kallen's place, that night three weeks ago, must have left him with a lacerated ego, and a touchy anger that took nothing at all to rouse. Suddenly, congested blood darkened his face; his eyes glittered with heat. And, as a curse tore from him, a balled fist swung without warning and took the prisoner squarely on the mouth.

Joe was knocked sprawling, spitting blood, but hurt less by the blow than from landing on the ribs scored by Bart Dolan's bullet. He heard the sheriff's quick protest, and then Slaughter was placing one of his big hands against Davis's chest, shoving him back as he said harshly, "Maybe you've forgotten, Sheriff! I got a score to settle here!"

Davis caught himself. He never seemed to know just how to treat this son of Morgan Slaughter's; now he exclaimed, "Don't it make any difference? Or, maybe nobody told you— this fellow just got through saving your father's life for him!"

"I'll bet!" The big fellow made it a sneer.

"It's the truth. And he killed a man doing it."

"A better man than *you* can ever hope to be!" Joe Elliott added bitterly.

He had pulled himself to one knee, and when he said this Slaughter loosed a roar of rage and charged as though intending to trample right over him. Joe tried to scramble out of the way. A heavy knee took him squarely in the chest and bowled him over, knocking the wind out of him; but when Slaughter moved to sink a boot into his belly, Joe had managed to roll aside.

Sobbing for wind, he fought to his feet. The man with the rifle reached a hand but he shook it off, saying savagely, "Damn you, let go of me!" And, really roused now, he waded in to meet Slaughter as the latter swung around, searching for him.

The big man's clubbed fists churned the air awkwardly, inexpertly. Joe avoided them with ease, as he had that night at Kallen's Bird Cage; he had the measure of his opponent and he waited until the man was in range. Then he brought a looping blow up from around his knees and caught his breath as hurt muscles stretched, and were jolted by the shock of the knuckles connecting.

Rick Slaughter was stopped in midstride. His arms spread helplessly and Joe sunk a fist into his soft middle, hit him again in the face. A sound of pain broke from the man; he backed away, his arms coming up to shield him.

"Even with a bullet hole in me, I can lick you!" Joe gritted. "And you know it!"

Nobody seemed to be trying to stop them, now—neither the sheriff nor his armed assistant. They watched as though stunned by the outburst of fighting; and down in the street the crowd stood motionless, too, while Slaughter's boots and Joe Elliott's thick-soled farmer's shoes raised a thunder from the boards of the broad bank stoop.

Joe crowded his enemy, saw Rick peer wildly around with blood leaking from a cut lip; he said fiercely, "No use hunting for Tod Grandy! Tod's dead—Reb Beecher killed him. Did you know that?" He couldn't tell from the expression of Rick's face whether this was news or not. What he did see was the beginning of terror, as Rick Slaughter realized nobody was going to step in and pull his enemy off him. And this craven show of fear tripped some kind of trigger in Joe Elliott.

His face a stiff mask, his whole body aching, he caught the big man and struck him right and left, cuffing him to his knees. The smell of sweat and fear rose from him rankly, as Joe seized Slaughter by his clothing and raised a menacing fist. "By God, now you're going to talk! You're going to tell why you and Grandy lied about me. You're going to tell us what the hell really happened that night . . ."

"Don't! Don't hit me again!" The words broke in bubbles of saliva, on the slack and trembling lips. "I'll tell. If you just won't hit me . . ."

Hands were grabbing Joe Elliott, hauling at him; he shouted in protest and clung to his enemy until Slaughter was dragged forward off his knees. "That's enough, Elliott!" the sheriff said hoarsely in his ear. "Do you hear me? Let go!"

It was only when Rick's shirt tore, with a sound of ripping cloth, that Joe loosed his hold and the big fellow went down heavily on his face. Panting, the hair streaming in his eyes, Joe saw then what had made the sheriff move at last: Morgan Slaughter stood in the door of the bank, a look of thunder on his blocky features. He stared at his son, and then at Joe who was being firmly held now. And Sid Davis said gruffly, "Sorry, Mr. Slaughter! They got in an argument and started fighting before I was able to stop them."

Morgan Slaughter scowled at the crowd in the street, he made an imperious gesture. "Bring them both back inside here. Hell, we don't need an audience for this . . ."

Joe Elliott's fighting fury had drained away, as quickly as it sprang into being. It was replaced by a bone-deep lethargy, his body protesting against the punishment bullet-torn tissues had been made to endure. He let himself be turned and marched again into the building, but he didn't manage to lift his feet high enough; in clearing the threshold, a toe caught and he would have been pitched headlong except for the hands clamped to either arm.

Then the doors were shut and he was being lowered onto a bench just inside. As his arms were freed he raised one and pushed a sleeve across his sweating face. With something of an effort he focused on the scene before him.

Circled by the sheriff and a half-dozen others, Morgan Slaughter stood facing his son. The two were about of a size—both big men, and with an obvious family resemblance; but when you saw them together like this you saw, even more, the differences. The father, though no longer in the prime of life, had the vigor and solid strength that the son would never have. There seemed to be something left out of Rick Slaughter's face, too, and out of his eyes. You didn't notice it so much, until you saw him confronted by the man he was meant to be modeled after.

Now Morgan Slaughter's face was like granite. He told his son, "I heard something very interesting out there, just now. I'm curious to hear more of it."

Rick was still breathing hard from the fighting. He tried to sound innocently puzzled. "I dunno what it might be, Paw. He said a lot of things. I reckon I'd of near killed him if you hadn't stopped me."

174

"I'm talking about something *you* said," his father answered coldly. "You were about to tell the truth about what really happened, the night you were robbed."

"I never said anything like that!" The young fellow tried to laugh it off, as he started to turn away. "You misheard."

An iron hand descended on his shoulder, hauled him back to face the danger in the old man's unyielding stare. "I heard fine! Now, suppose you tell me just what the hell you meant!"

"But Paw, I—" Rick's nerves crumbled; his whole face seemed to break up and fall apart. "I *had* to say it, Paw, to make him let me alone! Sheriff was just standing by—not doing a damn' thing . . ."

His voice trailed off, before the unwavering hardness in the older man's stare. Suddenly, wasn't a man here but knew, as Morgan Slaughter did, that the fellow was floundering deeper and deeper in a morass of pretense. And now the banker took his son by his torn shirt front and pushed him, hard, against the closed door, so hard that it shook and the timbers cracked explosively. Face inches from the younger man's, he said tightly, "Tell the truth—for once, if you can! If Elliott didn't jump you that night—then who did?"

Rick's mouth trembled. "It—it was Tod Grandy."

"*Grandy!*" Slaughter's eyes widened in utter disbelief. "By God, are you trying now to blame it on a dead man, that can't answer back?"

"No! No! It *was* Tod! I swear it!"

"But, you two were *friends!* You don't mean me to believe he laid open your skull with a gun barrel and lifted your roll?"

"I'm trying to tell you, Paw, if you'll just let me—if you'll just listen!"

The old man released him, dropping his arms. He took a deep breath into his barrel chest. "Tell it, then," he snapped.

"I couldn't, before—I wouldn't have dared. Tod said he'd kill me . . . He heard about my winning that night and he laid for me, only he didn't hit me hard enough and I seen

175

his face. So then he told me what would happen, if I gave him away. Said he'd always really hated me—I had it all, and he had to work for wages; and this was his way of getting even . . ."

Rick Slaughter put up a hand and pushed it through the thick, curling mane of yellow hair. The sweat and the pallor of fear made his face look sick. "But I'd let out a yell when he hit me, and I was bleeding like a stuck pig and people were running up from everywhere. We had to tell them something. Tod said, tell them it was Elliott that jumped me and he'd back me up. He even give me back half the money he'd took—"

"You cheap—lying—bastard!" Unable to contain himself, Morgan Slaughter lashed out with a clublike fist that took Rick squarely in the face and sent him staggering back into the door. "Because the kid had beat you in a fair fight, you let me hound him for a crime he never committed!" Trembling with fury, Slaughter drew a deep breath as he shook his head and put his look around at the others. "My son!" he exclaimed, out of bitterness and shame.

Rick couldn't meet the silent stares. He broke; with a sound that was almost a whimper he turned, fumbled for the doorknob and wrenched it open. He went stumbling out and no one tried to stop him.

Slowly, the big rancher turned then and looked at Joe Elliott, still seated on the bench. "You'll be letting this man go, of course, Sheriff."

Sid Davis hesitated. He rubbed a hand across the back of his neck. "It might be a little more complicated than that," he began uncertainly.

"Why should it be?" the big man snapped. "I'm withdrawing any charge I made against him. As for this robbery today—hell, we only lost about fifty dollars that we know of; and that'll probably turn up in the trash on the floor, once we sort it out." He gave a kick at the litter with one solid cowhide boot, scattering it. "I hear the Bart Dolan he killed was his own brother. All I know is, he stopped the man from killing *me*—and I'm ready to testify to that in court. Now, what the hell else you got against him?"

"He jumped parole."

"How do you know that?" Slaughter retorted, snapping the lawman up. "Just because he forgot to report to you a time or two, seems like a piddling sort of excuse for sending a man off to prison! Ain't he made himself a respected member of society, around here? Ain't he got himself a steady job?"

The sheriff started to open his mouth. Slaughter waved him to silence. "Oh, all right! So Quitman fired him. But he's got a job with me—any time he wants it. You hear me, kid? Any time at all. Come and see me and I'll find something for you to do." He looked around then impatiently. "Where'd that doctor get to? I want him to fix this boy up—give him the best treatment he can—just like he was my own son!" He looked toward the open door; his mouth hardened bitterly. "I only wish to hell he was!"

But then the banker shook his thoughts loose from that direction. He turned abruptly, with a shout for the teller. "Frank! Let's get the hell to work. We got to find fifty dollars somewhere . . ."

Then, somehow, Joe Elliott was seated beside the desk in the jail office, while Sheriff Davis fished a familiar-looking brown envelope from a drawer and pushed it toward him. "Here," the lawman said gruffly. "Check your belongings, make sure they're all there. After what you just been through, you should be in bed somewhere. But there's business that has to be taken care of."

"I'm all right." Numbed, chiefly, by the events of the past half hour; even the hurt of his wound could scarcely seem to break through the stunned reaction to the too-rapid shift and change of events. Joe stuffed the envelope into a pocket without bothering to open it.

Davis scowled at the desktop; as always in moments of uncertainty, he reached for his pipe. Holding it, he said, "I got a confession. I never did report you for jumping parole —seemed like such a damned final closing of the door! I guess I kept hoping you'd come back, of your own accord. That's the reason I got so rough with you today, when Quitman brought you in at the point of a gun. Disappointed, I suppose.

"Another matter," he went on, "that I almost hate to bring up: There'll be rewards for at least three of the men who were killed today. Including Bart Dolan . . ."

Joe Elliott's head jerked up; he stared at the lawman in horror. "You think, for even one minute, I'd want any part of—?"

"I know." The sheriff nodded. "But the money's there, for somebody to claim. Would you rather it went to that mob that grabbed your brother over toward Newton, after the train holdup, and then couldn't hold on to him? Ought to be something better to do with it than *that!*"

The young fellow hesitated, and then slowly he said, "I guess you're right, Sheriff. I'd like to see part go to buy him a decent burial, and a stone. As for the rest—there's a woman named Rose Lenson, on a farm near Augusta. I know she won't want to take the money; but she needs it bad for herself and her kids. She'll likely realize Bart would have wanted her to have it."

Davis took a pencil and made a note. "I'll see to it," he promised. "That takes care of the business."

"Thanks." Joe hesitated, and then said it again: "Thanks, Sheriff. That's not a word that comes very easy, to me. Looks like I may have lost that chip I used to carry around on my shoulder."

Before answering, Sid Davis picked up his pipe again, began to fill it from a pouch of rough cut. "Some things are hard to unlearn," he said finally. "You've had a rough time; but, it ought to go a little better, now. For one thing, looks like you can just about write your own ticket with Morgan Slaughter. He meant what he said about a job."

"Well, I just don't know." The young fellow looked at his big hands, that were bruised and aching from the fight with Rick Slaughter. "I suppose maybe he would try to make me one, if I asked him. But I don't belong on no ranch, or in a bank, either. I'm a dirt farmer, Mr. Davis. It's all I ever knew. It's in my blood—what I was meant for."

Davis nodded, and popped a sulphur match on a thumbnail. "That's all right, too. The bank's always holding good farm properties, that it takes in on mortgage forfeitures. I imagine Slaughter would be more than glad, if it's what you want, to fix you up with a deal at the best terms a man ever dreamed of getting." He put the match to his pipe, sucked fire into the bowl. Smoke began to pour from the lips set about the pipestem.

The hands twisted in Joe Elliott's lap. "That sounds pretty good," he admitted. "For later on, maybe. When I'm ready. But, right now—" He stood up suddenly. "Sheriff, would you think I was crazy if I said I want to go back to Quitman's?"

The other man stared; his face went blank. Slowly he shook out the match and dropped it on the floor, and took the pipe from his mouth. "Quitman's?"

Joe nodded. "If he'll take me, of course."

"You mean it? After the way he treated you?" The sheriff's eyes narrowed. He added shrewdly, "Or is it Mary you're thinking about?"

He nodded, admitting it. "But I'm also thinking the old man needs help, on that place of his—and that he's so ornery there's not much chance anybody else will stay. Maybe, too, I still owe him something. But at any rate I understand him

179

now; I know nothing he does can ever hurt me again . . . What do you think?"

"I think," the other answered slowly, "that this is a damn' sight more than the old hellion deserves! But, if you've learned that kind of patience and forgiveness, I reckon you won't go far wrong, whatever you do. Just don't forget to keep in touch with me. Remember, I'm still your parole officer."

"Sure," Joe Elliott said.

Holding himself very carefully against his injuries, he walked to the door of the jail, looked into the street that had pretty well emptied out now after the morning's high excitement. The bodies of the dead had long since been removed to a more decent place. You would hardly suppose that anything had happened.

Suddenly, though he still felt tired and hurt, there was also an inner kind of well-being. It was as though he had passed one of the hard peaks of his life. You could never hope to see very far ahead, but the road that lay just before him looked like an easier grade—a chance at least for a man to catch his breath, and get his bearings.

"I'll be seeing you," Joe told the sheriff, and walked out into the sunlight. Behind him, sitting relaxed at his desk, Sid Davis was already building up a cloud of blue smoke from that ancient, evil-smelling pipe.

D(wight) B(ennett) Newton is the author of a number of notable Western novels. Born in Kansas City, Missouri, Newton went on to complete work for a Master's degree in history at the University of Missouri. From the time he first discovered Max Brand in Street and Smith's *Western Story Magazine*, he knew he wanted to be an author of Western fiction. He began contributing Western stories and novelettes to the Red Circle group of Western pulp magazines published by Newsstand in the late 1930s. During the Second World War, Newton served in the US Army Engineers and fell in love with the central Oregon region when stationed there. He would later become a permanent resident of that state and Oregon frequently serves as the locale for many of his finest novels. As a client of the August Lenniger Literary Agency, Newton found that every time he switched publishers he was given a different byline by his agent. This complicated his visibility. Yet in notable novels from *Range Boss* (1949), the first original novel ever published in a modern paperback edition, through his impressive list of titles for the Double D series from Doubleday, *The Oregon Rifles, Crooked River Canyon,* and *Disaster Creek* among them, he produced a very special kind of Western story. What makes it so special is the combination of characters who seem real and about whom a reader comes to care a great deal and Newton's fundamental humanity, his realization early on (perhaps because of his study of history) that little that happened in the West was ever simple but rather made desperately complicated through the conjunction of numerous opposed forces working at cross purposes. Yet, through all of the turmoil on the frontier, a basic human decency did emerge. It was this which made the American frontier experience so profoundly unique and which produced many of the remarkable human beings to be found in the world of Newton's Western fiction.